A Short Stay in
PURGATORY

A L A T

RED FOX

A Red Fox Book

Published by Random House Children's Books
20 Vauxhall Bridge Road, London SW1V 2SA

A division of Random House UK Ltd
London Melbourne Sydney Auckland
Johannesburg and agencies throughout the world

Copyright © Alan Durant 1994

1 3 5 7 9 10 8 6 4 2

First published in Great Britain by
The Bodley Head Children's Books 1994

Red Fox edition 1997

Printed and bound in Great Britain by
Cox & Wyman Ltd, Reading, Berkshire

RANDOM HOUSE UK Limited Reg. No. 954009

Papers used by Random House UK Limited
are natural, recyclable products made from wood grown in
sustainable forests. The manufacturing processes conform to
the environmental regulations of the country of origin.

ISBN 0 09 913781 X

Contents

For Richard, Max, Madeleine, Jane, Sue, Sarah, Alison, all my friends then; and for Jinny, my best friend since.

Getting Away

She'd been standing on the hard shoulder for nearly half an hour when it started to rain. A hard, cold, heavy rain – the kind of rain, she thought bitterly, that always seemed to fall on Sunday afternoons in autumn, like this. It wasn't yet five o'clock but the daylight was almost gone and she found herself staring into a haze of headlights as cars approached and sped by her, showering her with dirty water.

At any moment, Dad will pull up and find me here by the roadside – soaked to the skin, pissed-off, beaten – and she almost hoped he would. But some small voice of defiance inside told her not to give in, to hold up her sign a little more boldly and give it another shot.

When the red pick-up pulled up, she thought it was all over. The great adventure. Dad had come on his red charger to rescue her. But when the door opened she saw, not dad's familiar, weather-beaten face, but the ginger hair and spectacles of a stranger.

'Going to see the Queen?' he asked, jauntily.

'What?' she said.

'London,' he said.

'London, yes,' she said.

'Hop in then,' he said.

She hesitated. She'd told herself she'd only accept a lift if there was a woman in the car or, preferably a family – never a man on his own. She wasn't that stupid. But this *was* a man on his own. So what now? If she let this lift go, who knows when she'd get another? The longer she stood by the roadside, the greater the chance that Dad or the police would come by and pick her up.

'I won't eat you,' said the man, smiling.

She stood motionless, peering into the pick-up's invitingly dry interior. *He looks harmless enough. But then don't they all?*

A great glob of rain landed on her neck and ran down her back under her clothes and in the end it was this bodily discomfort that decided her. She got into the pick-up and closed the door.

'Seal weather,' said the man, as the truck cruised along in the slow lane. 'That's what my sister Margy calls it. Flippin' seal weather. Too cold and wet even for the ducks.'

'Seal weather,' he repeated and glanced across at the girl, grinning broadly, as if seeking appreciation for the aptness of the phrase.

She duly obliged with a quick, on-off smile, from the mouth only. For her eyes were filled with disquiet. *I shouldn't have got in, I'm a fool. I might end up murdered in a lay-by somewhere.*

He seemed too attentive, too friendly. She wouldn't take off her wet coat as he suggested, but pulled it around her more tightly as if it were a

2

piece of armour. She said 'no' to his offer of wine gums. She kept her hand tensed on the door handle and tried to stay as far from him as possible. She responded in monosyllables only.

'Sorry about the smell,' he said suddenly and nodded towards a screwed up bundle of paper on the floor by her feet. 'I had chicken and chips for my Sunday lunch.' He pursed his lips and shook his head a little. 'Don't like chicken much. Not like that. A nice roast sometimes – Margy does a nice roast. But that stuff's all grease, isn't it? Slimy. What I like's a nice piece of cod.' He looked across at her as if he expected some sort of reply.

So she said: 'Yeah.' *This is stupid. I'll ask him to let me out at the next service station. I should never have got in.*

All about them, cars went hurtling past in the wet – everywhere people were on the move, on their way home from weekends away. Families . . .

'Yeah,' he said. 'Give me a nice big piece of cod any day. Or haddock. Or plaice. Or rock. Rock's nice. Margy doesn't like rock, though. It's the one fish she won't touch, rock.'

He pulled out to overtake a lorry and for a few moments the windscreen was opaque with spray.

'You had your lunch?' he asked, but didn't wait for an answer. 'You don't want to go to London on an empty stomach. Big place, London. Biggest city in the world as the crow flies. Not like Stanborough. Do you know what my sister calls Stanborough?'

A polite, pinched smile. *Keep him talking. Show*

some interest. As long as he goes on happily talking you'll
be all right. You'll get out of this pick-up unharmed.

'She calls it the biggest place in the world as the dodo flies.'

He laughed. It was more of a boyish snigger than a real laugh.

Like the sound of boys in school, at the back of the class. Boys laughing at things that weren't really funny, just to draw attention to themselves.

A picture came into her head of Denzil and Paul and Gofa with his stupid cap, the peak turned round the wrong way. And thinking of these familiar, everyday things filled her suddenly with a rush of relief. *Relax, girl. Calm down*. He was just a grown-up Gofa, this man. A small man from a small town. Boring. He wasn't going to harm her. She'd be OK. *Don't panic. You're starting a new life, girl. You're getting away. In an hour or so you'll be in the big city, away from all these little people. Piccadilly Circus, Leicester Square, Oxford Street . . . Life!*

'As the dodo flies,' he repeated, enjoying this idea hugely. He glanced across at her once more. 'Dodos are extinct, you see, so they don't.'

'Fly,' he added. 'She's got a sense of humour on her, my sister. She really has. I could tell you some stories.' He shook his head, grinning.

Oh God. He's not going to keep on telling me boring stories about his boring sister all the way to London, is he?

But he didn't start a story. Instead, he turned on the radio. There was a hum and a fizz, then the sound of a familiar jingle came from the back of the pick-up.

'Five o'clock,' he said. 'Top forty. I like listening to the charts. Music's a load of old rubbish mostly, but it's an institution, isn't it? Like Sunday tea. Margy can't stand it. She says pop music's an insult to five-year-olds. So I only listen to it when I'm on my own. Suppose you listen to it, don't you?'

'Sometimes,' she said, without enthusiasm. She never listened to the charts – except when she couldn't help hearing her sister's radio blaring through the wall. It was a part of the Sunday afternoon routine – a routine she hated. It was no accident that she'd chosen a Sunday afternoon on which to run away. When she got to London, Sunday afternoons would be over – for ever. Life would be one long Saturday.

Sundays really drove her crazy. That long, dull, final dead-end straight of the weekend that began with lunch and stretched through the evening to bed. Dad watching the football or a film or a game-show or anything on TV; Mum pottering about the kitchen, washing-up, baking, ironing, before she too was drawn to the television; Brian, her brother, out in the garage tinkering with his motor bike; Diane in her bedroom with the radio on, supposedly doing her homework, but more likely trying out some hideous new shade of nail varnish or eye shadow . . . And in every house in the street it was the same. The whole place was dead or busy with things that amounted to nothing. Sometimes she thought she'd

5

like to run up and down the street, rattling on the windows like Wee Willie Winkie, shouting, 'Let's do something! Why are you all so boring? You're wasting your lives.' But she never would. And anyway, she'd get no response. They were all corpses round where she lived. Dead-end people living dead-end lives. That was why she was getting away. Thank God she was getting away.

Her thoughts were interrupted by his singing – nasal, tuneless.

'I like this one,' he said, smiling and turned the volume up slightly. When the chorus came he sang along happily, with no inhibitions, as though he were on his own – the way her dad did sometimes when he was in the bathroom, safe behind a locked door. She felt embarrassed for him and wished he'd stop. There was nothing more embarrassing than wrinklies trying to pretend they were with it. Like teachers at school – Miss Young always going on about her favourite bands, what gig she'd been to. As if they could give a monkey's what she did with her weekends. As if they couldn't see she was just trying to win them over. Sugar the pill. The only people it took in were dirbrains like Gofa.

'Sounds brill, Miss Young,' he'd say – or something equally inane. And she'd say something like, 'Yeah, it was wicked.' And all Gofa's crew would laugh heartily. It made her want to throw up.

All of a sudden she really did feel very sick. Her face went flushed. She needed some air. She wound the window down a little and felt the cold, wet air whoosh in against her skin.

'You all right?' he asked. 'You look a bit iffy.'

She felt too sick to speak.

'That's travelling on an empty stomach,' he said. 'You want to eat something before you go on a journey. "You won't get far on an empty tank" – that's what my sister Margy says.'

It was the last straw. In her nausea and tension his words rubbed on her like a match against a matchbox.

'I don't care what your bloody sister says,' she snapped. 'Why do you keep going on about your sister all the time. I'm just feeling a bit car sick, okay.' She turned her flushed face back towards the open window.

He said nothing.

When she looked across again, she saw he was staring straight ahead, his head very still, his eyes seemingly mesmerized by the windscreen wipers. The only thing that moved was his Adam's apple.

'I been hurtin' so long, baby,' sang a plaintive voice on the radio. But without the sound of the man's voice, the pick-up seemed strangely, almost eerily silent. Having wished a moment ago that he'd shut up, now she wished he'd speak. She felt very young, very unsure of herself. Rather foolish.

I shouldn't have lost my temper. He's doing me a favour. He didn't have to stop and give me a lift.

'Look,' she said, 'I'm sorry. I really am. I shouldn't have snapped at you like that. I didn't mean that about your sister. You know what it's like when you're feeling sick, you, well... You know.' She looked at him with a pleading smile. But his eyes were fixed on the road ahead.

'Yeah,' he said, but without looking at her, 'I know. Never get like that myself, but I feel like it sometimes inside. Sometimes I want to shout. Sometimes when Margy... when she gets at me, you know. Has one of her moods.' He laughed a little, nervously. 'Then I really want to bellow.'

Suddenly, seeing this crack in his bluff exterior, her heart warmed to him. He didn't seem so old after all – he was approachable, sort of sweet. And there was, she thought, something very touching about his devotion to his sister.

'I'm always shouting at my sister,' she said. 'She drives me crazy – always pinching my things. I shout at her, she shouts at me, we slam a few doors ... It gets pretty noisy in our house.' For the first time since she'd left home that afternoon, she found she was smiling.

'Do you live with your sister?' she asked.

'Yeah,' he said, recovering some of his former heartiness. 'Like two peas in a pod we are. That's what Margy says. We've always lived together in the same house since we were babies. I was even born there. It's just the two of us now, since Mum and Dad died. We do everything together.'

'You must get on really well,' she said, thinking once more of her own sister, imagining her lying on the bed with the radio blaring, flicking idly through *Just Seventeen*, blowing now and then on her newly varnished turquoise nails.

'We went to Venice last year,' he said. 'You been there?'

'No,' she said. And suddenly it dawned on her.

She won't be lying on her bed reading, she'll be downstairs in the front room. They all will. Mum, Brian, Diane. They'll have read the note and be sitting by the phone waiting. Hoping I'll ring Dad or the police. Worried stiff. Mum with her arm round Diane. Brian all oily from his bike and Mum too concerned about me to tell him to go and clean himself up like she normally would.

'. . . We'd just arrived off the water bus,' he said, 'and we were in the hotel reception, and this chap comes down the stairs – American tourist I should think he was – blowing his nose like a fog horn. Margy frowns a bit, then she looks at him and says, "I see you've settled in nicely. You've unpacked your trunk completely!" '

His pale face turned towards hers again, momentarily – his eyes full of amusement, prompting her to share in the joke. But her stomach suddenly felt too small for the weight it was carrying. Her palms were damp with sweat. For the first time, she wondered: *When I get to London, what the hell am I going to do? I don't know anyone there. I've no qualifications. I'm fifteen, I've never even been away on holiday on my own before.*

'You can't beat family,' he said.

'No,' she said. 'No.'

9

And she really meant it.

'You know,' he said. 'You remind me a bit of Margy. How she was. As a girl.'

But she was in a world of her own. Back home.

When, a couple of minutes later, she caught sight of the sign warning of approaching Services (half a mile it said), she knew, without even having to think about it, what to do.

'Look,' she said. 'I need to make a phone call, urgently. Would you mind stopping at these next Services? I won't hold you up, I promise. I . . . well, the thing is, I've decided not to go to London after all.'

He was fine about it – very nice. Actually seemed a bit sad she was going, and she thought how ridiculous it was that she'd ever been afraid of him. He drove her right up to the door of the complex, though she said that by the petrol would be fine if he wanted to be on his way quicker. He didn't ask for an explanation, but she thought he deserved some sort of one.

'I don't think I'm quite ready for London yet,' she said. 'Maybe in a couple of years.'

'I'll give your regards to the Queen, then, shall I?' he said, as she got out.

'Yeah,' she said. 'Thanks. Thanks a lot. Not just for the lift, but, well, for helping me see things.'

He nodded. 'All part of the service,' he said with a smile.

For a moment, with the artificial light falling on his untidy ginger hair and specs, she had the impression he could almost have been her age. 'Boyish' her Mum would have called him. Behind his glasses, his eyes almost looked tearful. Instinctively, she gave him a warm smile.

'I think your sister sounds brill,' she said. 'Really great. You're very lucky.'

She slammed the door shut.

'Thanks again,' she called.

She waved as he drove away, but he didn't look back. For a moment she wondered where he was going. He wasn't the London sort somehow. Then she turned up the collar of her coat, picked up her bag and went to phone.

In the phone booth, she took a moment to compose herself. The decision to make the call had come spontaneously; actually making it, even though she knew it was the right thing to do, was a lot more difficult. What would she say?

Well, she thought eventually, *whatever I say I'll sound stupid. So I may as well get on with it*. She started to press out the familiar number, glancing as she did at the newspaper a previous caller had left behind. It was one of the tackiest Sunday tabloids. The headline read BUTCHERED! BROTHER SOUGHT IN SISTER'S SLAYING. Idly, as she punched the last digit, she turned the paper over to see the rest of the front page. Her finger froze on the button.

She stared, open-mouthed, unable to take in what she was seeing. In her ear, the drmmm drmmm, drmmm drmmm of the ringing tone. Looking closer now, horrified, as it sank in: the photograph, the description – a man with ginger hair and glasses, driving a red pick-up . . .

There was a click in her ear and an anxious female voice from faraway saying, 'Hello . . . Hello . . . Marie? Is that you, Marie?'

And then she broke down.

Pebbles

You've been waiting for this all week. When the bell rings, you're up like a rutting stag, bounding to the door. A quick peck on the cheek, 'See you later, Mum,' and then, bag slung over your shoulder, you're out the door and into the street. The heat hits you. The sunshine is of the mercilessly glaring variety and the air almost untroubled by breeze. You put on your shades, climb on your bike and follow the others out onto the road.

The trip takes around half an hour and you chat a bit about what's to come with Sam and Matt, but not that much because the road's pretty busy and noisy and often you have to go in single file. When you come to a quieter stretch, Sam says he reckons there's going to be a game of beach football – boys against girls. Raf's organizing it, he says, and raises his eyebrows. Matt grins and so do you, not because you're amused but because mention of Raf immediately brings to mind Jess which, in turn, fills you with a delicious tingling. It's the thought of seeing her that has made the prospect of this particular outing so exciting.

You're crazy about Jess. You've been crazy about

her for months and it's been agony all that time because she's been going out with Raf. Every time you saw them together you were wrenched by conflicting emotions: euphoria because you were so mad about Jess and desolation because she was with someone else. But last Saturday night Jess and Raf broke up. They are together no longer and suddenly the way is free. You know she likes you – you hope she fancies you – and today is your perfect opportunity to impress. And, boy, do you intend to impress. You've even bought new swimming trunks for the occasion. You studied yourself wearing them in front of the mirror last night and they looked pretty good. 'James Dean, eat your heart out,' you said – and you meant it only half in jest.

You think about Jess as you cycle. Into your mind's eye comes her willowy, elegant body, enhanced by curves; the way her long blonde hair falls about her face; the beautiful clearness of her blue eyes; the softness of her voice . . . The heat and effort inflame your desire, and by the time you arrive, red-faced, sweaty, you cannot wait to see her.

But she's not yet there. A few of the others are gathered down to the left of the small jetty where they said they'd be, but (and of course you're a bit disappointed, but only momentarily because the delicious thrill of anticipation quickly returns) Jess is not among them. To your surprise, though, Raf is. You thought he'd stay well clear of places where Jess was likely to be after their bust-up, but he's there all right, dark hair flopping under his cap, with a T-shirt that reads 'I Am The Big'. Not 'The Big I Am', but 'I Am The Big'. This strikes you as a typical piece of Raf exhibitionism. The sort of thing that gets him noticed and admired and for which in the past you have often envied him. But not any more. As he greets you noisily, you mentally attach the word 'loser' to his slogan.

He does not seem like a man bowed, however. Far from it. He is as chirpy – cocky even – as ever. He does not even flinch when Jess's name is mentioned, but just shrugs.

'There're plenty more pebbles on the beach,' he pronounces dismissively and, as if to emphasize the point, he picks up a handful and lobs them into the air. They drop with an almost silent thud into the wet sand. You hope he might elaborate and tell you exactly why Jess no longer finds him irresistibly attractive but, alas, he is not forthcoming. Instead, he grabs a Frisbee, dances across the sand and gets the afternoon's sporting activities under way.

Frisbee-throwing is followed by a lengthy splash-about in the sea, during which you have to endure some ribald ribbing about your new trunks – mainly from Raf ('Did you have to pay extra for the codpiece?') – and an attempted debagging. You take it happily. You can afford to be generous, nothing can rile you today. You feel completely carefree. Jess will soon be here – and, as ever, simply the thought of that awakes a pleasure strong as the waves that are rising and falling about you. You plunge into one, as it crests, and feel the surf slap invigoratingly against your chest. Shaking the water from your hair and eyes you see that Raf and Sam, each with a girl on board, are about to commence a piggy-back water-fight. You join in with the cheering spectators.

Back on dry land, you sit with the others, as Sal, who is always good for a laugh, tells a story about something that happened at her school. It involves a small furry animal, a scalpel, some test tubes and a teacher who is universally loathed. His nickname is Ratty and she has mentioned him on a number of occasions before. The story is an amusing one and affords plenty of opportunity for audience participation. Normally you would be one of the major participants, but today you are too preoccupied to do more than echo others' comments or join in the laughter.

You are starting to become slightly uncomfortable, impatient. You've been at the beach for over an hour now and there's still no sign of Jess. It is only the fact that her friends Brid and Ruby haven't turned up yet either that stops the panic setting in. It's unthinkable that *none* of them will come, so you reckon it's a pretty fair bet that they will all appear together. This thought keeps the pot of anticipation simmering nicely.

Your mind wanders from the beach to an anonymous love poem you sent Jess, about a month ago, when the agony of your unspoken passion grew too great to bear. You wonder if she guessed it was from you (she's given no indication that she has), thinking that you hope she did, but with a nagging little suspicion somewhere at the back of your head that it might be better if she didn't. In the poem you compared her with a siren and yourself with Ulysses tied to a mast begging to be allowed to go to her, unable to resist her incomparable charms. The words struck a note of desperate adoration that pleased you immensely – so much, in fact, that you hoped that Jess might show the poem around to her friends, so that they too could be impressed by your eloquence.

Someone else is relating an anecdote now about a couple of teachers, who were apparently caught having a steamy affair in the boiler room – and then Raf chips in with a story about one of the lab assistants at his school who was discovered between the pages of a sexy woman's magazine, totally naked, and showing abnormal interest in a shower attachment. This is a characteristically Rafish story and, you suspect, almost certainly untrue, but it is told with such swaggery energy and conviction that everyone laughs as much as if it really were true. Everyone except you, that is, for the sound of the others' voices suddenly irritates you, as too does the unrelenting sunshine. You cannot bear to wait any longer for Jess to arrive. But there is still no sign of her.

You get up and go down to the edge of the water. You move in a few steps to allow the waves to flow in over your feet and ankles, then drag back your toes, feeling the gravelly surface scrunch beneath

17

your soles. An ironic cheer goes up behind you . . . and you jump and your heart leaps, because you know that someone has arrived. Finally the moment you've been waiting for all week is here. Jess has come. But when you turn, it is Brid and Ruby you see and, as one desperate instant's eye-search reveals, *only* Brid and Ruby. Jess is not with them.

Brid is wearing a wide-brimmed straw hat with a colourful floral ribbon that immediately makes her the centre of attention. She takes the hat off, shaking out her long bright red hair, and passes it round for various members of the party to look at and comment on. You join them, just as Raf removes his baseball cap and puts on the straw hat, posturing ridiculously. Ruby smiles at you and you give a quick smile in response, but your thoughts are all on Jess. You are dying to ask about her, but cannot, for fear of betraying your feelings for her. You have to wait for someone else to say something, and, eventually, thank goodness, Sal does.

'Where's Jess?' she asks. She says it casually, like she might be asking someone if their cold's any better. To you, though, the question is as crucial as, 'Tell me, doctor, how long have I got?' You hold your breath, as you listen to the reply – which seems a long time coming, or maybe it's just that it takes a long time to seep through the shell of your traumatized brain.

'Oh, *well*,' says Brid sort of theatrically, 'she's not coming.' Those three small words are enough to flatten your spirits, as surely as a massive foot trampling a sand castle, but it's obvious from Brid's expression that there is plenty more to come. She settles herself down on the sand, Ruby beside her – and the story she tells does not break your heart (broken parts, after all, can be mended), it shatters it completely, utterly.

The night before, Jess, Brid and Ruby went to a party and Jess got off with some guy. He was a student, Brid says, quite a lot older than them. He was also very clever and witty and had the most fantastic eyes. Brid wouldn't have minded at all getting off with him herself, only she was already with someone else who, incidentally, turned out to be a bit of a jerk and just wanted to wrap his tongue round her tonsils all night. In the midst of your misery you suddenly catch sight of Raf and wonder how on earth he can look so cool. Either he is putting on an amazing front, or he really doesn't give a damn about Jess any more. You find this possibility incomprehensible. It appears to be true, though, because as you watch, Raf pulls a face and makes some lewd comment to Brid, which results in her chucking a handful of wet sand at his navel.

'Anyway,' Brid says, to conclude her tale, 'Jess's gone to some concert with this guy this afternoon, at his college.'

And that's that. The day lies in ruins around you. And not just the day, but your whole miserable life. It was bad enough when she was going out with Raf, but at least you knew him – and you knew his flaws. You could even feel sort of superior to him at times. But against this new super, older guy, you're nothing. You have no chance. But the worst thing of all is that Jess didn't even show up this afternoon. If she'd arrived with this new guy it would have been bad, but the feeling of abandonment her not turning up at all has instilled in you is truly, utterly terrible. You wish you could bury yourself in the sand and die.

You become dimly aware of activity around you and realize that the others are preparing for the game of beach football that Sam had talked about earlier. Raf is organizing goal posts, while Brid and Sal and a couple of other girls have an hysterical kick about. There is nothing in the world that you feel less like doing at this moment than playing a high-spirited game of beach football. So you get up, mumble some excuse to Matt, who is standing nearest you, and quickly walk away, before anyone really notices that you've gone.

Once you judge that you're far enough away to be left in peace, you slow down, and your tread becomes a sort of shuffle along the waterfront. Your eyes stare down at your feet, watching them churn up the wet, spongy sand, as you go. You seem to be incapable of doing any more than just observing, as though your grieving mind is too shocked to think. But you can feel all right and the sorrow, anguish, tears through you, like rocks ripping through the sea. You come across a dead crab, lying upturned on the shore, and are struck by the symmetry of its many curved arms and legs. It reminds you of a

Hindu goddess – Shiva you think her name was – that you saw a picture of once in a RE lesson. The sight of the crab is somehow so arresting that you stop and sit down on a rock nearby.

The tide is going out now, leaving the dead crab behind with various other debris – a plastic lemonade bottle, dollops of drying seaweed, a damp, splintery plank of wood . . . and you, of course. Because that's the way you feel right now, like a piece of debris that the out-going tide has left behind. It's an image that might prove useful later in a poem, but at the moment it gives you no pleasure whatsoever. It merely symbolizes your misery.

You get up again and walk to the water's edge, watching the waves roll in, falling, slowly but surely, ever further short of you, and your eyes are drawn to the bed of wet pebbles that the retreating waves reveal. You are struck by how much more impressive and attractive they are than their dry, grey counterparts higher up the beach. The water gives the bedded pebbles a kind of sheen that makes them sparkle and brings out their colours – green, blue, brown, grey, orange, red, pink . . . You've never really noticed before how colourful pebbles are. They are all different shapes and sizes too. Each one is distinct, individual, you realize, if you look close enough – just like people. And you remember what Raf said earlier about there being plenty more pebbles on the beach.

Bending down, you pick up a pebble that is rounded and that, with its pattern of lines, reminds you of one of those satellite shots of the earth. You hold it in your hand a moment then toss it away and it plops into the water. Then you pick up another shaped like the handle of a gun, look at it, and toss that away too. Finally, your hand finds what it has been searching for. A stone that is slim, smooth, elegant, blonde . . . You turn it over in your hand for a moment or two, feeling its cool, marbly curves against your palm and fingers. Then, impulsively, you throw it out into the sea and watch it skip away across the waves, into the haze.

It's an Ill Wind . . .

I was pissed off with Rich that night. I'd been pissed off with him since Thursday evening when he'd phoned to say that his sister was coming to the party, so he wouldn't be able to stay over after all. It was supposed to be our first night together. We'd had it planned for weeks – ever since Steff had announced that her parents were going away and she and Tim were going to have a party.

It was just the opportunity I'd been hoping for. Rich and I had been going out for well over a year and it felt like time to consummate things. Necking and that's all right, but it can be bloody frustrating. We were both still virgins and the way Rich kept dithering about it, it seemed like we might be for ever – until this party came up and the invitation to stay the night. And now Rich had backed out.

He'd been very apologetic. But his sister, Carrie, had heard about the party and she wanted to go. She knew Steff wouldn't mind. The more the merrier was Steff's philosophy – as long as they weren't troublemakers, like Calvin and his crowd. The problem was that as Carrie was only fifteen, Rich had to be responsible for taking her and bringing her back. Otherwise their parents wouldn't let her go.

'So, what's the problem?' I said. 'She doesn't go.'

'It's not that simple, Suze,' said Rich. 'Mum's putting mega pressure on me to take her.'

'Didn't you tell her you were staying the night?' I asked.

There was a heavy silence at the other end of the line.

'You didn't tell her, Rich?' I said.

'I was just about to,' he said, 'when this problem came up.'

'Rich,' I said, 'you've known about this party for weeks.'

'I was waiting for the right moment,' he said.

'The right moment,' I repeated. 'You've really blown it.'

'I'm sorry, Suze,' he said. 'There's nothing I can do. I was looking forward to it just as much as you, you know.'

'Yeah,' I said. I could've cried, I felt so disappointed.

'We could still, you know, do it,' said Rich. 'We don't have to stay the night. We could go off somewhere together at the party.'

'No,' I said. 'I don't want it to be like that. Not the first time. I want to spend the night with you. That's what we arranged. Besides, it's going to be a great party. I don't want to get there and then disappear off into some bloody bedroom for the whole of it, thanks a lot.' For a moment I'd been on the verge of saying that I wouldn't go – but it really was going to be too brilliant a party to miss. So I expressed my anger instead by hissing, 'Well, I hope you're bloody pleased with yourself! Goodbye!' and then slamming down the receiver before he had a chance to reply.

It wasn't even as though I didn't like his sister. Quite the opposite. Caz and I got on very well – even though she was a year younger. She was pretty mature for her age and had a very good sense of humour. But there are times when three is very definitely a crowd – and this was one of them. I loved Rich. I was crazy about him. I wanted to sleep with him. It's not like I was a sex maniac or anything. I just wanted to sleep with Rich because I loved him and he loved me and it felt like we were both ready. When I thought of us doing it, how it might feel with him inside me, it sent a shivery thrill through my body – and I'd been thinking about it a lot. In bed, on the bus, in class . . . And now, it was not to be. I wanted to scream.

When Rich came to pick me up on Saturday evening, the atmosphere was decidedly frosty. I wasn't as mad with him as I had been – I'd had a couple of days to get over the disappointment a bit – but I wasn't going to let him see that.

'You look nice, Suze,' he said.

'I look awful,' I said. 'I've got bags the size of footballs. How can you say I look nice?'

'I like football,' he said. Then realized he shouldn't have. 'I just think you look nice tonight,' he said.

'Unlike usually,' I said, 'when I obviously look ugly as a pig.'

'Suze,' he said, 'come on. You know what I mean.'

I just sort of grunted as I put on my coat and then marched out to the car. Caz was sitting in the back.

'Hi, Suze,' she said enthusiastically.

I got in and slammed the car door. Rich hated me slamming the car door. He said I'd damage the lock. The car was an old Fiat and barely roadworthy. We drove off in icy silence.

I needed Rich to warm me up a bit, to try and draw out my bad mood – he'd have taken some flak, but I'd have come round in the end. He hardly said a word, though, the whole time we were in the car, which just allowed my ill feelings to build up again. By the time we reached the party, I'd decided I wasn't going to speak to him, even if he deigned to speak to me. There were going to be plenty of other people to talk to anyway – including quite a few friends I hadn't seen for a while. I didn't need Rich . . . That's what I thought anyway. But when we got inside there weren't many people there – and I hardly recognized any of them. None of my friends was there.

'Where is everyone?' I asked Steff.

'Oh,' she said, 'they'll probably turn up later – after the pubs shut.'

'I think there's another party on too,' she added vaguely.

Steff's a nice person, but she's not the world's greatest party organizer – and this time she'd really screwed up.

After nearly an hour, still none of my friends (the ones I'd really been looking forward to seeing) had showed up and my mood had got really black. I'd had such high expectations of this party – and it hadn't fulfilled a single one of them; it was like Christmas all over again. I hate sitting in a corner at parties, not talking to anyone, but there wasn't anyone there that I really wanted to talk to – and I was hardly in the mood for jumping up and forging new friendships. Some people get themselves into a party mood by having a few drinks but I don't like alcohol and fizzy water hardly has the same effect. So I sat on the sofa with Caz, who made occasional unsuccessful attempts to draw me into conversation before she buzzed off to the kitchen. Rich, as usual, was in the thick of things; he was chatting with a group of guys from his school. It didn't look as if he was enjoying it that much, though, which gave me some sort of perverse satisfaction.

I was watching him (out of the corner of my eye so that it didn't look as though I was paying him any attention at all) when his face creased up in a sort of grimace. Then a couple of moments later it happened again – only more pronounced this time.

I thought maybe he was playing around, the way Rich often does. The others took him seriously, though, and I heard one of them ask him if he was OK. He was bent over now, holding his stomach. He said he was going to sit down and came over and slumped on the floor next to me. I didn't think there was really anything the matter with him, but I couldn't ignore him. So I asked him what was up – but not too sympathetically.

'I don't know, Suze,' he said, straining as if he was in a lot of discomfort. 'I've got this sharp pain in my gut. Just indigestion probably.'

I offered him my water and he took a drink. Then he took a deep breath. In the space of a few moments his face had lost its normal healthy colour. He looked grey and it was obvious he wasn't well. I got off the sofa and crouched next to him.

'Do you want to go?' I asked.

He took another deep breath. 'I don't think I can move,' he said. 'I feel too ill.'

I put my hand round his neck, lightly. 'Where does it hurt?' I asked. He put his hand low down on his waist, on the left-hand side. Then he looked at me, really mournfully – the way my kid brother does sometimes, when he needs reassuring about something – and he said: 'That's where the appendix is, isn't it, Suze?'

My heart went out to him. Rich has got a kind of phobia about his appendix. He had a friend who died of peritonitis and he's always afraid it might happen to him.

'Is it that bad?' I said.

'It's pretty bad,' he said, pathetically.

'Maybe we should go to Casualty,' I said. 'Just in case.'

Quite a few people had gathered around now, including Steff and Caz, who'd returned from the kitchen.

'You all right, Rich?' said Steff.

I explained to her what was up. When I mentioned appendicitis, Caz pulled a face, like 'Oh no, not that again.' But she and Steff both agreed that Rich ought to go to Casualty. He really was looking bad now. The problem was that neither Caz nor I was old enough to drive and Rich was in no state to do so.

'We'll have to get a cab,' I said. But I wasn't that happy about it because you can wait for ages on a Saturday night. Steff said she'd see if anyone else had a car and could take us. She came back a few minutes later with a tall black guy that I didn't know.

'This is Andy,' Steff said. 'He hasn't got a car, but he can drive and he says he'll take you up to the hospital in Rich's car.'

Knowing how Rich felt about his car, I also knew he wouldn't be very keen on this suggestion.

'It's only insured for me,' he said, through clenched teeth.

Andy smiled broadly. 'That's okay,' he said. 'My insurance'll cover it. And anyway, I'm not gonna have an accident.'

There was no way Rich was going to relax at the

prospect of some stranger driving his car, but by now he was in too much pain to veto the proposal. This was an emergency. So Caz and I helped him out to the car and Andy followed along behind.

'This must be the special pygmy model,' said Andy, trying to squeeze his long legs in under the dashboard. Rich found it difficult enough, and he was about six inches shorter. The seat catch was broken and it didn't go back as far as it should have done. Andy turned on the ignition. For once, the car started fine.

'Casualty here we come,' he said. 'Hang on in the back there, man, we'll soon have you there.'

He ground the car into gear (I could feel Rich's wince without being able to see it), released the handbrake and we roared out into the road. He seemed to have got the impression that this was a real life-and-death, full-throttle emergency – either that or he'd been watching too many car chases on TV – because he drove like he was on a racetrack. It was all racing and sharp braking and screeching round corners on two wheels. By the time we got to the hospital I was feeling ill, never mind Rich. Andy beamed.

'We made it,' he said, as though there might have been some question of us not doing so.

'Yeah, thanks a lot, Andy,' I said.

'What took you so long?' said Caz.

Andy beamed even more.

'Do you want me to go in with you?' he asked.

'No, it's okay,' I said. 'We might be some time.'

'Yeah,' Andy agreed. 'I suppose so.'

'Specially if they have to operate,' said Caz, who didn't seem to be taking the whole thing quite as seriously as the rest of us. Rich moaned – whether in pain or in dismay at the mauling Andy had just given his precious car, I'm not sure. Caz and I took an arm each and led him into Casualty.

I don't know what Casualty's like usually, but that Saturday night it was pretty crazy. More than half the people in there were drunk for a start. There was one guy with a makeshift bandage round his head who kept shouting obscenities at no one in particular; another guy was lying stretched out on the floor, snoring. We had to step over him to get to the reception desk and give the woman Rich's details. She listened without any apparent concern, asked a couple of questions, then told us to go and sit down until Rich was called. She didn't know how long that would be. Saturday night was always very busy, she explained, especially after the pubs had shut.

'He's in a lot of pain,' I said.

She just pursed her lips and said a nurse would be over to see us as soon as possible.

'Perhaps you should fall on the floor and writhe about a bit,' Caz suggested. 'Or faint.'

'This isn't funny, you know, Caz,' I said. 'Rich might be seriously ill.'

Rich's face turned white as a doctor's coat. 'Thanks, Suze,' he murmured.

The guy with the bandaged head shouted another

obscenity, then got up and lurched towards the exit. He crashed dramatically through the swing doors. For a moment everything was quiet. Then a woman's scream shrieked out from one of the rooms behind the desk. It was the kind of scream you could imagine coming from someone who was being brutally tortured.

'No! No!' she cried.

I looked at Rich and Rich looked at me.

'Maybe we should just go home,' he said. 'It's probably nothing.'

'We may as well wait now we're here,' I said.

'Who wants to go home?' said Caz. 'The party's just getting going.'

'He's having a good time anyway,' she added, nodding towards a bench seat over in the corner, where an old tramp was sitting, seemingly quite oblivious to the hubbub around him, enjoying his own little cheese and wine party.

Half an hour went by and I was getting pretty agitated. A nurse came over and asked Rich a few questions, but then she disappeared back into the torture rooms again and we were just left sitting there, waiting. In the meantime a number of people came and went. One middle-aged man was rushed in on a trolley, having suffered a suspected heart attack. He walked out a few minutes later, looking pretty sheepish, with his arm in a sling. His wife said he'd pulled a muscle in his shoulder. Caz thought this was hilarious; she was practically having a heart attack herself she was laughing so much.

Rich was smiling too. But I was annoyed that some-one with such a minor complaint should have been seen before Rich, who might have been dying for all they seemed to know or care. I went over to the desk and made my point, indignantly, to the woman. I could have been talking to the speaking clock for all the reaction I got. She said they were doing their best and repeated that someone would see Rich soon.

I went back to my seat, really fuming, to find Caz and Rich still giggling about what had happened.

'It's not funny,' I said angrily. Suddenly, to my surprise, I could feel myself on the verge of tears. Everything had gone wrong: my planned first night with Rich, Steff's party and now this. It was all too much. All out of control.

Then Rich doubled over, clutching his stomach, and groaned. I put my hand on his back.

'Are you okay, Rich?' I asked anxiously, then looked around quickly to see if there was a nurse or anyone about that I could call.

For a moment, Rich stayed as he was. Then, letting out a kind of sigh of relief, he straightened up again. His face had got a lot of its normal colour back and bore an enormous grin. I was about to lay into him for getting me all worried ... when I caught a whiff of the most diabolical smell. It was truly gruesome – like bad eggs. Caz gave out an exclamation of disgust and turned her head away. Rich looked at her, then he looked at me.

'I think it was just really bad wind,' he said. 'It

feels much better now I've got it out.' He stood up and started pacing up and down. The awful smell lingered in his wake. Caz was trying to hold her nose and laugh at the same time.

'Rushed to hospital with a suspected fart,' she said. I looked up at Rich happily striding around the room and, for the first time that evening, I started to laugh too – and with the laughter, all my frustration, disappointment and tension seemed to find a release, the way Rich had when he'd let off.

'You are an idiot, Rich,' I said to him when he came back and sat down. 'Are you sure you're okay now?'

'Sure, Suze,' he said. 'Let's get out of here.'

'Father and turd doing well,' quipped Caz.

I went over and told the woman on the desk that we no longer needed to see a doctor because the problem had righted itself.

'It was just wind,' I told her. 'A really enormous fart,' I added, enjoying the expression of distaste that came across her usually blank face. Then I joined Caz and Rich and we walked out, leaving the old tramp to consume his cheese and wine in peace.

Rich dropped Caz off, then took me home. It was well after midnight by now.

'It's a bit late for you to come in, I suppose,' I said regretfully.

'I suppose so,' Rich agreed.

'Otherwise I'd happily fix you a late-night snack,' I said. 'You know, beans on toast or something.'

Rich closed his eyes in a kind of mock grimace.

'Don't you start,' he said. 'It's bad enough having to put up with Caz. Father and turd doing well . . . He shook his head. 'I'll never live this down.'

'No,' I said.

I knew he wasn't really worried. He wouldn't mind the story being told, because when it was he'd be the centre of attention – and there was nothing Rich liked better than that. It was one of the things that attracted me to him. He was vague, indecisive, maddening sometimes – but he was a lot of fun and very caring too. He looked at me now with a tender expression.

'I'm sorry about tonight, Suze,' he said and he put his arm out for me to cuddle up to him – which I did. 'You really do look lovely,' he said.

'Mmm,' I purred, putting my head on his shoulder. We sat like that, in silence, for a few minutes, with Rich gently stroking my hair. I felt tired, but very, very happy. Then Rich said, 'Suze?'

'Mmm,' I said sleepily.

'I've got something to tell you,' he said, still stroking my hair.

'What?' I asked, yawning.

He waited an instant, then he said, 'My parents are going away for the weekend in a couple of weeks' time.'

It took a couple of moments for this information to sink in. Then I raised my head up so that my chin was on Rich's shoulder. I didn't have to say anything; I just smiled and so did he, then he dropped his head towards me until our lips met. And then I was reminded of another thing that I liked about Rich.

A Short Stay in Purgatory

The other guy was older. A real man. Twenty-five, maybe, with long hair framing a tough, cunning sort of face, ears punctuated with earrings. He was lying, smoking, on the top bunk, propped on one elbow.

'First timer?' he asked. But the youth didn't answer. He sat with his head in his clenched hands, staring down at the stone floor. The man looked down at him with a leery smile. He took a long drag of his cigarette. Then exhaled, coughing.

'Jesus!' he exclaimed. 'These effing things are all tar. That's the last time I cadge a fag off a pig.' He coughed again. 'You don't smoke, do yer?'

The youth said nothing – gave no indication that he'd even heard the question. Into the heavy silence came the muffled pitter-patter of rain.

'Talkative sod, aren't yer?' said the man. 'You ain't in court now.' He drew another puff from his cigarette and screwed up his face in distaste. Then he sat up and looked across at the youth's hunched form. Carefully, he laid the cigarette butt on his palm, took aim and flicked it at the youth. It fell by his feet, but he didn't look up.

'Oi, dumbo,' said the man. 'Cat got your tongue? I asked if you've got a fag?'

The youth didn't reply. But, very slowly, with a kind of pendulum precision, he shook his head.

'Ah,' said the man. 'We have life!' He sniggered, then started to cough. Outside, the rain continued its steady pitter-patter. The man stared at the youth for a moment, then he turned round to face him fully, swinging his legs over the side of the bunk.

'Look, mate,' he said. 'Let me give you a word of advice. I don't know what you done or how long you're in for, but if you want to get out in one piece then you're gonna have to liven up a bit. You sit there all day, saying sod all and not answering anyone when they talk to you, and they're gonna get right pissed off. And I'll tell yer, there's some right ugly monkeys inside. I should know,' he added, 'I've been in enough.

'Do you know how old I was when I first did time? Fourteen,' said the man. 'They put me in this effing home place. Home! It was more like prison than prison . . . I've been all over, I have. Done it all. Cars, burglary, drugs, assault. They got me on armed robbery this time, the bastards. All I did was drive the car. I reckon I'm better off inside.' He paused reflectively.

'Where yer going then? Maybe I can put a word in for yer . . . Ask them not to gob in yer porridge.' He laughed throatily again.

The youth remained motionless.

'Christ, kid,' said the man. 'Yer might as well

37

cheer up, because it's gonna get a whole lot worse before it gets any better. Just like the economy.' He laughed again.

Inside the darkness of the youth's thoughts a single memory burned. The day he was eighteen. Came of age. Became a man. Killed. Died. His whole life formed and shattered in a matter of moments . . . The rain, more insistent now, seemed to be drumming against his skull. The man's voice started up again, discordant as the untutored scrape of a violin.

'Just leave me alone, can't you?' the youth cried and clenched his fists even tighter about his head.

The man swore and hawked up phlegm from his throat. He made as if to spit, but then swallowed instead. He pushed the hair back off his face.

'Kids,' he said. 'Why'd they put me in with a kid? What did yer do? Nick some granny's handbag?' He pulled his feet up onto the bunk again and lay back on the pillow with his arms underneath his head. The next time he glanced down, the youth was looking down at something, held in his palm. Something that flashed gold in the fluorescent light.

'What yer got there? A cross?' asked the man.

The youth shook his head. 'It's a crucifix,' he said.

'Same difference,' said the man. 'You religious then?' Without waiting for a reply, he continued, 'I don't believe in none of that crap. God and all that. I don't know how yer *can* believe it with all the stuff that's going on today. God's certainly never done sod all for me anyway.'

'Maybe you've never given him a chance,' said the youth, quietly.

'What effing chance has he given me?' the man insisted. 'You tell me . . . None. Forget about God, mate. The best thing yer can do with that crucifix is swop it for something useful when yer get inside. Get yerself some stuff. What's it made of anyway?'

'Gold,' said the youth dully.

'Gold!' said the man and whistled. 'Yer better watch out the screws don't nick it then. They'll try and take it off yer – yer can be sure of that. They'd take yer effing soul off yer if they could find it.'

'They'd be welcome to it,' said the youth, closing his hand over the crucifix.

The man swung himself down on to the floor. He stretched and yawned noisily. Then he perched himself on the bottom bunk. The rain's patter had now become a persistent thud.

'How long yer in for then?' the man asked.

The youth stared at him, but what he was looking at was another man. His stepfather, standing, with an expression of amazement, his hand on a patch of red spreading across his checked shirt, just below his chest. Then the beads of blood at the corners of his mouth an instant before he fell.

'For ever,' he said.

The man grinned. 'Everyone feels like that the first time,' he said. 'But, what with remission and stuff, well, you'll soon be out. They're only too glad to see the back of yer, these days. Except heavy villains like yours effing truly of course. They want to throw the whole effing book at me. Bastards!' He put his hand to the pocket of his denim jacket as if reaching for his cigarettes. Then, remembering that he had none, he let his hand fall.

The youth got up from the bench and walked over to the door. He gripped the bars with both hands and squeezed himself tight against the door. In the blackness he could see his mother's face, scared, pleading, one eye almost shut – and his stepfather's foot above her, threatening, his breath heavy with fury. Then, almost soundlessly, his tensed body barely quivering, the youth started to sob.

The man stared at the youth's back. He snorted and then coughed, looked embarrassed. He made as if to speak, but then thought better of it or no words came. He slumped back on the bunk. Outside, the rain began to pour. Minutes passed.

The youth turned around and faced the man. 'Do you believe in hell?' he said.

The man ran his hand through his hair and inclining his head slightly, said, 'I told you. I don't believe in none of that crap. Heaven, hell, God . . . If he did something useful – like get me a decent fag, for instance – then I might believe in him.'

'You don't understand,' said the youth, turning again to face the bars. 'You don't understand at all.'

'I understand what I need to understand,' said the man.

For a couple of minutes, there was silence again between them. Beyond the cell walls, thunder rumbled, presaging a storm. Then the youth turned from the door and walked over to the man, his eyes looking down at the floor. He opened his hand, revealing the golden crucifix – pushed it forward, offering. Without raising his eyes, he said to the man, 'Take it. I want you to have it.'

The man pulled himself up on his elbows. 'What do you mean?' he said, bewildered. 'Are you crazy?'

'Take it,' the youth insisted. 'It's no use to me now, where I'm going. You have it. You can use it.'

He dropped the crucifix on to the bunk beside the man – and in the split second it took to fall, he recalled everything. The way drowning men are supposed to in the instant before death.

It was his eighteenth birthday. He'd come home from school and was sitting in the kitchen, drinking a celebratory glass of sparkling wine with Mum. His stepfather had come in, drunk as usual, abusive, jealous of their happiness, their faith. Mum, angry, had stood up to him and, as so often before, he'd hit her, hard, in the face. Then his stepfather had hit him too when he'd tried to intervene. Knocked him back. Said something about him being a man now and that he could take a man-sized beating. Then he'd turned on Mum again, knocked her down. Laughed at her pleading, his breath heavy with fury. Said this time he was going to show her who was God – stamp his authority on her. Raised his foot . . .

He'd shouted at his stepfather to stop. Threatened him – and then panicked when he'd seen the older man coming towards him, his big fist hard as a club, his eyes full of hatred . . . turning suddenly to shock when the knife went in. And then the blood came. He felt the chopping knife in his hand, but didn't remember picking it up. Then his stepfather fell and it was all over. For ever. The waters closed over him.

Through the beat of the rain came the sound of footsteps approaching. The cell door opened and two dark figures stepped in.

'Glad you could make the party,' said the man, cheerily. 'But where's your bottle? Oh, don't tell me you haven't brought a bottle.'

'We've got plenty of bottle, Franky,' said the first policeman. 'We must have, to come unarmed into a cell with such a hard bastard as you.'

The man laughed his phlegmy laugh. 'What, no truncheons? No sand in a sock? No knuckle-dusters? Just going to kill me with your smell, eh?' He screwed up his face in disgust and put his hand over his nose.

'We're not interested in you, Franky,' said the first policeman.

'Your time'll come,' said his companion.

'Promises, promises,' said the man.

The first policeman raised his hand in front of him and beckoned the youth.

'Come on then, son,' he said. 'Let's be havin' you.'

Without a word, the youth walked slowly over towards the door.

'Better watch out for that one,' said the man,

gesturing towards the youth. 'He's got a terrible tongue on him. Never stops.' He grinned.

The youth didn't turn round. He shuffled out through the cell door, followed by the two policemen. On a small window in the corridor, opposite, he could see the hard rain running, and superimposed on it, for an instant, like a hologram, the stern face of the judge.

'See you in hell, mate!' the man called.

'What's this one in for?' said the second policeman, when they were out in the corridor.

'Manslaughter,' said the first policeman.

'How long?'

'The minimum. Three years.'

The second policeman clapped his hand on the youth's shoulder. 'Who's a lucky boy, then?' he said.

The Star

It was Christmas Eve and it was raining. The atmosphere at home was anything but seasonal. My dad and my older brother Tom had just had a massive row, ending up with Tom grabbing his coat and slamming out into the street and off to his girlfriend's for the rest of the day. I was feeling pretty miserable. I'd never been so close to Christmas and felt so totally untouched by its spirit. In a desperate attempt to find some goodwill, I decided to cycle round to see Jemma. Jemma's house was always cheerful – especially at Christmas.

Jemma was a friend from church. Her dad was the organist. He was a very jolly man with a beard and eyes that twinkled behind his glasses. A real Father Christmas. It was he who opened the door to me.

'Ah, Alastair,' he said with a smile. 'Come in, come in. Compliments of the season and all that. Jemma's in the sitting room.' He waved me through with an expansive sweep of his arm.

The sitting room was very festive. There was lots of holly and mistletoe; an open fire was burning and on the mantel shelf above it home-made decorations sparkled. In one corner of the room stood an enormous, very beautiful tree. It must have been about eight feet tall and bright with lights, lametta and baubles. It was a far cry from the pathetic artificial effort we had at home. Jemma was standing on a chair by the tree with a large silver star in her hand.

'Hi, Ali,' she greeted me. 'You're just in time to witness a MacKenzie family ritual. The placing of the star.' She reached up towards the top of the tree, but even stretching she was a few inches short.

'It looks like you need a hand,' I said.

'I think you're right,' she agreed. She looked across at her father. 'Daddy used to lift me up, didn't you?' she said. 'Before I got too old – or he did . . .' Her words tailed off teasingly.

'Who's too old?' her father said and he stepped over and put his arms around her waist and, with a big grunt, lifted her the couple of inches she needed to place the star on top of the tree. She wobbled for a moment and squealed and I thought maybe she was going to crash into the tree. But it was just her father kidding around. When he let her down again, he was gasping melodramatically. 'I think you're right, Jemma, I am too old,' he said. 'I need a drink after that.'

Then he offered us one too. Jemma persuaded me to have a glass of ginger wine.

'It's really Christmassy,' she said.

Sitting in that cosy room, chatting to Jemma, with a glass of ginger wine in my hand and a disc of Christmas carols playing in the background, my spirits began at last to rise a little. Jemma's enthusiasm for Christmas was so great that it would have been impossible for anyone not to have been affected by it. She even looked Christmassy with her green eyes and long red hair.

'I wish it were like this round our place,' I said and I told her a bit about the various unseasonal goings-on in our household. She nodded sympathetically. She was a good listener, Jemma.

'Maybe they'll all suddenly get into it when tomorrow comes,' she suggested.

'Maybe pigs might fly,' I said gloomily.

Jemma and I talked a bit more and I helped her put up a few decorations and then her mum came in and had a chat and offered round some mince pies and her dad sat down at the piano and played a couple of carols and we all joined in . . . It was very jolly. How Christmas Eve was supposed to be, I thought. Anyway, it made me forget about all my grouses for a while. Cycling home again though, through the dingy dampness of the early evening, they soon returned – and got stronger when I walked through the front door to hear Mum and Dad bickering about the turkey. It wasn't going to be a good Christmas.

I went to midnight mass that night, but somehow it had lost its power and meaning for me – and, when New Year came, I gave up going to church. Also, the new crowd I got in with at school thought Christians were wet and priggish and seriously unsexy. Jemma phoned me a couple of times to find out what had happened to me and I made some lame excuses about why I hadn't been to church and said I'd see her soon. But she was pretty busy with her music – she played in several orchestras – and I got more and more involved with my new gang, and we lost contact. I didn't see her at all for nearly two years. During that time I went to lots of parties, had a number of short-lived relationships, bought myself a motor bike, nearly got expelled from school for severe slacking, made and changed friends several times, spent the whole of Christmas intoxicated and didn't really think about my faith at all. I didn't mock religion like the rest of the crowd, I just didn't talk about it.

When Christmas approached, I found I was actually looking forward to it, as I hadn't for a couple of years. The atmosphere at home had improved since my brother Tom had left – especially now that I'd come through what my mum called my 'wild period' – and everyone was a lot more relaxed. There wasn't a lot of excitement about the place, but at least that meant that no one was expecting too much.

It was while at a loose end on Christmas Eve – I'd wrapped my presents and there was nothing worth watching on TV – that I started to think about Christmasses gone by, and my thoughts turned to Jemma. I had a yearning suddenly to visit her. It would be nice, I thought, to be able to reciprocate some of that seasonal good cheer she'd shown me in the past. We could have a real celebration. Phoning might be a bit awkward, I reckoned, as we hadn't seen each other for such a long time, so I thought I'd surprise her by just turning up on her doorstep. I got on my bike and cruised round.

I knew there was something wrong the moment Jemma's Dad opened the door. I didn't expect him to kill the fatted calf on the spot, but I did expect him to show a little pleasure in seeing me. Just a smile of recognition. But there was nothing. His face was blank, his eyes devoid of that warm twinkle that I remembered.

'You've come to see Jemma?' he inquired dully.

'Yes,' I said.

'I expect she's in the sitting room,' he said and then turned into the house and walked off, leaving me to find my own way in. I was shocked because he'd always been so polite and hospitable in the past. I had a fleeting thought that maybe he didn't approve of motor bikes and had taken offence at my leather jacket and helmet. A fair number of adults did – parents especially. But the problem, I soon realized, went much deeper.

I got my second shock when I opened the sitting room door. I'd expected Christmas cheer to shine out from a sea of sparkling decorations, a roaring fire and a splendid tree. But there was no fire, hardly even a Christmas card, never mind a decoration, and the tree in the corner was small and bare. Jemma was sitting on the floor, staring into a large card-board box. She looked up fiercely when I came in – then, gradually, a smile appeared on her face.

'Hi!' she said enthusiastically and got up to greet me.

'How are you? Long time no see.'

She'd changed. Her hair was cut short in a bob and she looked a lot older than when I'd last seen her. But then, of course, two years had passed.

'You had me worried for a minute,' I said. 'I thought you were going to bite my head off.'

'Oh,' she said dismissively. 'I thought you were *him*.'

'Who?' I said, puzzled. 'Your dad?'

'Yes,' she said. 'If you can call him that.'

'What, have you fallen out or something?' I asked, totally bemused.

'You could say that,' she said. Then she told me all about it.

One day, about six months before, Jemma's dad had announced that he was having an affair with another woman. And not a quick fling either with some young thing, but a relationship with a woman of his own age that had been going on, secretly, for several years. Not surprisingly, the news had come as a real shock to Jemma and her mum. Jemma despised him and didn't want to have anything to do with him, but her mum relied on him a lot and didn't want him to leave. And it seemed like he couldn't make up his mind just what he wanted to do. He stayed with his family half the time and with his mistress the other half. As far as Jemma was concerned, though, he'd gone, deserted, and she wouldn't talk to him unless she absolutely had to.

He was no longer her father – their relationship was over.

It was just about the saddest thing I'd ever heard. I'd known Jemma – and her dad – a long time. Years. Their loving relationship had been one of the few things in life that I'd felt I could take for granted. Hearing about its break up was like finding out that your house was built on sand.

'I hoped he'd gone off to his woman,' Jemma said. 'I don't want him skulking around here all over Christmas. It'll be miserable enough as it is.'

'But you were so close,' I said.

'Yes,' she agreed. 'Tragic, isn't it? But then I didn't know what kind of man he was then, did I?' She looked wearily at the cardboard box on the floor. 'I suppose I ought to get these decorations put up,' she said. 'Although it hardly seems worth the bother somehow. There'll only be me and Mum and neither of us feels much like celebrating. I can't wait for it all to be over to tell you the truth.' Hearing such a confession from Jemma's lips – Jemma who'd always been so into Christmas – was really shocking.

Heavy footsteps sounded on the stairs and a moment or two later, the front door slammed.

'Thank God for that,' Jemma said. 'He's gone, the silly man.' Her words were hard but I could sense she was close to tears. I wanted desperately to say something comforting, but I couldn't think of anything that wouldn't just sound crass. So I changed the subject. 'Look,' I said. 'Why don't I give you a hand putting up the decorations?'

She shrugged. 'If you like,' she said, without enthusiasm.

While we worked, I gave Jemma a brief sketch of what I'd been doing over the last couple of years and she talked a bit about her life. And while we were talking, she was a lot more like her old self. But it was only a brief flurry, like when you shake one of those kids' bubble decorations and make a little snowstorm. As soon as there was a silence, I could see her spirits sink.

After about half an hour, we'd done quite a good decorating job. The room wasn't a patch on how I'd remembered it from the last time I'd been in the house, but it did look Christmassy. Even the spindly tree looked quite jolly. We hadn't been able to find any lights for it but, buried at the bottom of the box, I discovered a silver star. And I recalled the ritual I'd witnessed before.

'Aren't you going to put this up?' I asked.

'Oh, that old thing,' said Jemma. 'It's about time we threw it out. It's terribly shabby.'

I looked at the piece of foiled card in my hand. Jemma was right, it *was* shabby – the foil had started to come away on some of the points, a couple of which were badly creased. I smoothed them out carefully, affectionately.

'You can have it, if you're so attached to it,' Jemma said with dark amusement.

'Are you sure you don't want it?' I asked.

'Positive,' said Jemma. 'It reminds me of *him*. Take it or chuck it. I don't want it.'

So I took the star. Looking at it gave me a warm, nostalgic feeling – it reminded me, I suppose, of the festive cheer I'd found at Jemma's in times gone by. Besides, we didn't have a star on our tree at home – just a really tacky plastic fairy that I hated. I wished, though, when I left Jemma's, that I'd been able to give her something in return – something that might make her feel better, some clever or wise words that might help her make sense of what she was going through. But I couldn't. My only consolation was that at least she seemed more cheerful when I left than when I'd arrived – even though I suspected her smile would quickly disappear once she'd closed the door behind me.

I went to midnight mass that night. Jemma wasn't there and nor was her father, but it was they who dominated my thoughts and because of them, the service had a new kind of poignance. There was one reading, in particular, that made a special impression. I'd heard it countless times before, knew it almost by heart, but now it seemed to take on a new resonance. It was the passage from St Matthew about the arrival of the magi.

Now when Jesus was born in Bethlehem of Judaea in the days of Herod the king, behold, there came wise men from the east to Jerusalem saying, where is he that is born King of the Jews? For we have seen his star in the east, and are come to worship him. . . .

And lo, the star, which they saw in the east, went before them, till it came and stood over where the young child was. When they saw the star, they rejoiced with exceeding great joy.

These words were still singing in my head as I sat alone, in the peace of the sitting room at home, early on Christmas morning. I was looking at the illuminated tree topped by Jemma's star. I was glad I'd put it up. Even slightly battered – maybe even *because* it was slightly battered – it was a beautiful thing somehow. It was like a symbol of faith: the light in the darkness that, no matter how lousy things appear to be, promises something wonderful – exceeding great joy. It was there for shepherds and wise men, near and far, young and old, happy and sad, betrayer and betrayed . . . It was there even when we weren't.

I wished suddenly that Jemma had been there with me. I wished I could have spoken to her, tried to comfort and reassure her. Because I knew, in that moment, what I wanted to say. I wanted to tell her that no matter how battered, how crumpled, how worn it might seem, the star would always shine. Jemma, your star will always shine.

Hayley Initiates

'First day he comes in, right,' says Hayley, 'we all thought what a plonker. He had these sort of nylony brown slacks on and a jacket with huge lapels, right, and a really gruesome swirly patterned tie. You know, like someone had puked on it.' She squinted and wrinkled her nose. 'It was flared, too – like a mutant kipper. And he had specs as well and little shifty sort of eyes that wouldn't look at you and really horrible hair. Nearly as bad as his,' she says nodding at one of the boys in the group around her. The others laugh and the boy gives Hayley the finger. She grins and wrinkles her nose again. Then turns once more to the new girl. 'Anyway, he was new – this was his first school, right – and we always try it on a bit with new teachers. Try and suss them out like – you know, let them know who's boss.' There's a ripple of appreciative laughter.

'Anyway, we do the usual stuff, right. All the boys move their tables to the back of the class, all the girls come up the front. Me and a couple of the others get really close and stare at him, all sort of gooey-eyed—' (she demonstrates) '—you know, like he was fantastically attractive and we'd just love to get our warm, nubile young hands on him—' (sniggers) '—which was a real effort considering how *totally* repulsive he was. But, anyway, right, I think he must have been blind as a bat, because he doesn't take any notice of us, even though we're staring right at him. I mean you'd expect him to look embarrassed or deliberately try to avoid our eyes or something, but he just looks right through us, like we weren't there. I hate that. So in the end I put my hand up and I ask him if I can be excused – and now he has to look at me, but his eyes are still shifting about, right.' She rolls her eyes around ridiculously and the others cackle. 'And he says, "Why?" And I look at him, pinning him with my eyes, so that he's got to look at me, and I say, "Well, sir, my period's starting." Whoosh, his face goes a beautiful shade of scarlet and, of course, as soon as I say the word "period" all the boys start to groan and the girls laugh and suddenly the whole class is in uproar. It was magic.' She shakes her head with amusement and the others grin broadly. The new girl smiles too, though without their conviction – she wasn't there after all.

'Anyway,' Hayley continues proudly, 'we knew we had him after that, right. He just couldn't cope with us. He didn't even really try half the time. I tell you he was a really weird bloke – I mean all teachers are weird, right, but this guy was really weird. He just stood up the front talking to no one in particular, just sort of burbling on, you know, while all around him people were calling out to each other and throwing things and moving their tables about . . . Every time he turned his back to write something on the blackboard, one of us would get up and leave the room. And we weren't exactly quiet about it. But he never said a word. Wei-erd.' She rolls her eyes again, then wrinkles her nose.

'It was a real laugh that week,' she says, addressing the new girl. 'A real riot. You could do anything, right. Lee there—' (she flicks her head at one of the boys) '—he brought in his dad's mobile phone, right, one day, and while the lesson's going on, he's sitting there phoning up pop-call and one of those telephone sex places. And then I said, "Order me a pizza for lunch, will you?" And Lee says "Right you are". Then he starts going round the class, yeah, taking everyone's orders – Ham and Pineapple, Four Seasons, Hot Chilli . . .' She flicks out her tongue snakily and licks her lips. 'He even goes up to old Gonzo, you know, and asks him. But Gonzo just ignores him and goes on burbling away about I don't know what. Well, maths, I suppose, but it could have been Outer Mongolian basket-weaving for all we cared . . . Like I said, he was weird.' She contorts her face once more to emphasize her assertion, coaxing a smile from the new girl.

A hooter sounds and the new girl stirs, but Hayley puts a restraining hand on her arm. 'There's no hurry,' she says firmly. 'It's only Felps.' She wrinkles her nose and then adds with a sort of knowing sneer. 'We're always late for Felps.' The others murmur confirmation. The new girl hovers awkwardly.

'Anyway, listen,' says Hayley eagerly. 'I haven't told you the best bit, right – you know, about old Gonzo. The "denouement" as Boggo would say.' She says the word in an exaggerated imitation of their English teacher's West Country accent, which once again draws sniggers from the others.

'Anyway,' Hayley continues. 'It was the end of the first week, right, and we were all sitting there wondering what to do next – 'cause it seemed like we'd just about done everything we could. And I'm watching old Gonzo at the blackboard, chalking up figures and stuff, reaching down now and then to use the duster, but never looking away from what he's writing, like a robot or something, and all of a sudden this idea comes to me.' She claps a hand to her forehead comically. 'Sophie and Cathryn and Lisa and me all move our desks together in a kind of huddle and I undo my bra at the back and then sort of slip it off, you know, wriggling it down the sleeves.' Her sinuous demonstration provokes some ribald reaction from the boys, which she acknowledges with a grin and one raised finger. The new girl casts an uncomfortable glance in the direction of the school entrance, as Hayley continues. 'Then I scrunch it up in my hand and I get up and go out the front to the blackboard. I stand really close to Gonzo and I point to some figure on the board and ask him some stupid question about what it means. But while I'm talking, right, I feel for the duster behind my back and replace it with my bra. Gonzo doesn't notice, of course, because he's too busy ignoring me and chalking up new numbers on the board. Then I go back to my seat and wait for the fun.' She pauses for a moment then raises her hands as if to hold her audience's attention.

'A couple of minutes go by and then, bingo, he puts his hand down and picks up the bra and starts to wipe the board with it. Well, the whole class just erupts, you know. Mega laughter. Everybody's just falling off their seats. It's magic.' Her eyes are watering with amusement. 'Old Gonzo stops wiping and just sort of freezes. Then he glances at the bra in his hand and he goes really tense, like any moment he's going to absolutely explode, right. But he doesn't. Do you know what he does?' She shakes her head incredulously. 'He just drops the bra and walks out of the room. Just like that. Gone. And that's it, right. He never came back. That was the last we saw of him. Though Lisa reckons she saw him later, outside the school, you know . . . crying.' She pulls a mock tearful expression as the others jeer triumphantly. Then she joins in with their laughter. The new girl glances about her at the amused faces and smiles weakly.

At last, they walk back into the school building, already late for their next lesson, Hayley and the new girl arm in arm. 'That was brilliant that week. Really great,' says Hayley happily.

The new girl says nothing. She looks ahead a little anxiously as she walks, feeling Hayley's arm around her own, Hayley's arm and her arm, like links in a chain.

The Queen of the Ruck

The party was hot. The latecomers had finally arrived from the pub, bearing plentiful cans of lager. Good cheer was as thick in the air as cigarette smoke. Someone put an old Motown classic on the turntable and suddenly the sitting room was transformed into a dance floor. Bishen removed his trousers.

By the drinks table in the kitchen, two young men stood, looking on through the open doorway at what was happening. They were both about eighteen and burly, though one was considerably taller than the other. The tall one, Steve, shook his head and grinned.

'That Bishen,' he said.

'Yeah,' said Nick, the other. 'I don't know why he doesn't just come in his boxers.'

'He probably will later,' Steve said with a leer.

Nick laughed half-heartedly, as though his mind was on other things. He took a swig of beer and then put his hand to the top pocket of his denim jacket for his fags. He took one out, then looked from the packet to Steve and back to the packet quizzically.

'I'd offer you one,' he said finally, returning the pack to his pocket, 'but I've only got two left to last the rest of the evening. As it is I'll be gasping.'

'Mean bastard,' said Steve mildly. 'What about all those fags I gave you on rugby trips?'

Nick put the cigarette in his mouth and patted his jacket in search of matches. 'I said "thank you", didn't I?' he said. He looked perplexed for a moment. 'You couldn't give me a light, Steve, could you?'

Steve shook his head again. 'You've got a bloody nerve, Nick,' he said. But he handed over his matches. Nick lit up.

Steve twisted a can of lager free from its plastic holder. He snapped back the ring-pull and took a swig. Then he belched loudly. 'It's like piss this stuff,' he said. In the other room the stereo was playing I Heard It Through The Grapevine.

'I wonder what old Bish'll do,' mused Steve.

'Mmmm,' said Nick. He took a long drag of his cigarette then exhaled slowly, and the smoke came out in a kind of sigh. 'Do you ever wonder, Steve,' he said, 'what we'll all be doing in, say, ten years time? I do. Take Bish for example. I reckon he'll be a secondhand car salesman or something like that. Something sort of shady, but not exactly illegal.'

'A male stripper in a seedy night club maybe,' Steve suggested. 'Or maybe a drag queen. I've always suspected he's a woofter on the quiet, old Bish.'

'Really?' queried Nick. 'What ever makes you think that?'

'I don't know,' said Steve. 'Just something about him . . .' He grinned broadly. 'Not interested in rugby, is he?'

For a long moment, Nick contemplated the cigarette smoking between his yellowed fingers. And in that moment he nearly came out with it. What he'd been wanting to say. But something held him back – surprise perhaps that the opportunity had so neatly presented itself – and the moment passed.

'Nor's Casanova,' he said, referring to one of their contemporaries who was even now, it had been rumoured, upstairs with a member of the opposite sex.

'No,' Steve agreed. 'He's just a prat.'

Nick took another drag on his cigarette. He looked through at the dance floor, crowded with his peers – guys he'd grown up with over seven, eight years. Guys he liked, guys he didn't like, guys (by far the largest group) he was completely indifferent to. Most he'd never see again. He thought about that – and wondered whether it pained him at all. And found, to his surprise, that it did, a little. He couldn't help feeling curious about how they'd be in the future. In ten years a lot of them would be established in their chosen careers, married or in a long-term relationship of some kind. Quite a few would have kids. And these thoughts did get to him. Other people's futures seemed so much more appealing and less complicated than his own. He was brought back to the present by another loud belch from Steve.

'You know, Nick, the first thing I'm going to do when I get to Portsmouth is sign up for the rugby team.'

He crushed the empty lager can in his hand.

'We had some bloody good times, didn't we?' he said slowly, nodding his head for emphasis.

'Yeah,' said Nick, without any particular enthusiasm.

'The King of the Ruck,' said Steve appreciatively. 'How you got that ball out so often I'll never know. You were brilliant. There was one game, about three years ago, when we went on that Scottish tour. Do you remember?'

Nick nodded. 'I remember that tour,' he said.

'I'll never forget that game,' said Steve. 'We played some poncey Edinburgh college. And every single ruck, every single bloody ruck, you came out with the ball. It was incredible. Bloody incredible. That's when we started calling you The King.'

'The King of the Ruck,' he said again. 'You going to play at Leeds? What kind of team have they got? Any good? I suppose they're more into League, though, up there, aren't they?'

'I suppose so,' said Nick.

He remembered that tour very well. He'd thought about it a lot. But not for the reasons Steve thought about it. Nothing to do with the rugby. He'd never really liked rugby much anyway. He'd just been quite good at it, that was all. It had been a way of making himself 'normal' too. All that macho stuff. But he'd never really liked it. He'd rather have been sketching or painting any day. Any feats he'd performed on the field during that Scottish tour didn't mean a thing to him. It was what had happened off the field that stayed in the memory. Late at night, in the small room he was sharing with Minnow, the team's scrum half. It was his first time with a boy or a girl. He was fifteen. It had been done quickly in the dark. He couldn't exactly recall now how or why it had happened. It just had. And it had been good enough to make him feel bad for a long time afterwards.

Looking back, he knew he should have admitted there and then that he was gay. Admitted it to himself at least. Instead of going on for all this time with the charade of heterosexuality. Dating girls, even holding down a steady relationship with one for over a year. Making himself seen to be sexually active with the opposite sex. Most of them seemed to find him pretty attractive too – so the charade hadn't, on the face of it anyway, been that hard to maintain. Inside, though – that was what counted. And he'd been empty. Empty or unhappy, depending on how much of his real desires he allowed himself to acknowledge.

He'd pushed it aside at first as a kind of continuation of the kind of early adolescent homosexual flirtations that everyone went through. It had only happened just the once after all. But Minnow kept apart from him after that and gave him looks like he *knew* what Nick was about – and he, Minnow, wasn't into it. But Nick was still attracted to Minnow. He fancied him more than he fancied any girl. But he refused to admit it. He didn't want to be gay. No way did he want to be gay. It was the last thing in the world he wanted to be. So he threw himself into heterosexuality like others around him threw themselves into football or drama – hoping that after a while it might become natural, enjoyable even. But on the few occasions he'd had sex with a girl he felt a kind of despair, never happiness. A despair that he wasn't ever going to change and that was the way he was going to be for his whole bloody life. A woofter.

Nick looked for an ashtray to stub out his cigarette. In the end he made do with one of the many plastic cups strewn on the table.

'That's disgusting,' Steve complained. 'Someone'll want to drink out of that later.'

'They'll live,' said Nick casually. But he took the cup over to the bin and chucked it in. 'No one's going to drink out of it now,' he said.

'They should drink out of the can, anyway,' Steve conceded. 'No self-respecting bloke would want to drink beer out of one of these poxy cups.'

'Unless he's a woofter,' said Nick and, for once, saying the word didn't make him feel uneasy. It didn't make him feel anything. It didn't mean anything. He took a swig of lager and looked through into the sitting room. All those couples dancing. Heterosexual couples. There had to be some others like him, though, didn't there? Among all those people. But who? Surely he should have been able to tell – being one himself. But he couldn't. Apart from Peter Potter – "Fairy" to the rugby crowd – and Sean, who camped it up like a couple of drag acts. No way did he want to be associated with them. There had to be some 'normal' gay guys, surely.

'I'm going for a piss,' Steve said.

Left on his own, Nick reached for his last cigarette. A girl he didn't know came out into the kitchen to get a cup of water.

'Wow, it's hot in there!' she said and gave Nick a big smile.

'Yeah, it looks it,' he said in a way that wouldn't encourage further conversation.

The girl drank back her cup of water and left. Nick lit up. He felt apart from everything tonight. Not just these end of term celebrations, but everything. He was alone, although not unhappy. And then all of a sudden it sunk in that this wasn't just the end of a term, nor even the end of a year, it was *the end* full stop. He'd left. School was over. He was never going back. He didn't have to see any of these people again if he didn't want to. He didn't even have to see Steve again. In fact, he realized, he almost certainly wouldn't. He inhaled deeply, and for a moment felt elated, great. He was going away, starting anew, coming out. When he got to Leeds he wouldn't have to pretend anything. He could just be himself. It would, he thought, be like discovering sex again for the first time – but more fulfilling and without the guilt. He could put his adolescence behind him and start afresh. He could be really himself.

When Steve came back into the kitchen, he seemed surprised to see Nick still there.

'Thought you'd be in there raving it up,' he said, reaching for another can of lager.

'Someone's got to guard the booze,' Nick said with a grin.

Steve snapped back the ring-pull on his can.

'I just had a great idea, Nick, while I was in the bog,' he said. 'I think we should have like a rugby team reunion. Maybe arrange a match against next year's school fifteen. You know, have some drinks and a meal after. It would be a good excuse for a piss-up anyway. What do you think? Eh, buddy?' He put his arm around Nick's shoulder and dragged his head down, then started to move them both forward as though they were going into a ruck. 'Drive! Drive, pack!' he grunted.

And for an instant, there in the warm, smoky kitchen, the memory of so many wasted afternoons spent out on muddy playing fields and in all kinds of weather conditions came back to Nick. Along with the smell of damp boots and damp bodies. And the feel of his head burrowing in between backsides as he took his place at the back of the scrum or dived into another ruck. What would they have said, all those guys, if they'd known what a rugger bugger he really was. Not The King of the Ruck at all, but the Queen. The Queen of the Ruck.

Steve took his arm away to take another drink. 'Seriously, though, Nick,' he said. 'What do you think? It's a brilliant idea, isn't it? We'll murder 'em.'

Nick took a long thoughtful drag on his cigarette. Shall I tell him? he thought. Tell him now and get it over and done with.

'I think we should wait and see how things go, Steve,' he said. 'I mean we could be really busy in our first terms. Involved with our own activities and stuff. Why don't we just wait and see.'

'Yeah, I suppose you're right,' Steve agreed.

The music had got smoochy now, the cue for some serious pairing off. Bishen, now minus shirt and trousers, was the only single dancer left. And even he had a partner of sorts – he swayed about the dance floor clutching a carved wooden toucan.

'Look, Steve,' Nick said. 'There's something I ought to tell you.'

He fiddled with the cigarette, rubbing it back and forth between his fingers.

'What,' said Steve. 'No, don't tell me. You've been signed up by Wasps, you bastard.'

'No,' said Nick. 'No. It's—'

He looked deep into Steve's face, looking for any sign that he might have started to suspect what was coming, any sign that he might understand. But what he saw was a large, boorish sort of face, slurry eyes, cropped hair – the face of a rugger bugger, not the face of a soul mate. And it made him feel sad because, despite everything, Steve had been his friend.

'It's just that I don't think I'm going to play any more rugby,' Nick said quickly. 'I want to concentrate more on my painting and stuff.'

'Painting!' Steve scoffed. 'Painting. Sounds like you're turning into a bloody woofter,' he said. Then he grinned. 'You'll change your mind,' he said, 'once the season comes round again.'

Nick said nothing. He took a last deep drag on his cigarette, drawing it up as far as it would go, like he was drawing up his whole life, school, everything that had gone before. He blew the smoke out slowly, very slowly, in a thin stream, until there was nothing left to exhale, and then he reached down and ground the cigarette out. It's almost over now, he said to himself. It's almost over now.

My Weekend with Gandy

To say I'd been driving my family mad would be like saying Cyrano de Bergerac had a bit of a conk. The simile's particularly apt, because it was the said Cyrano who was, in part anyway, the cause of my condition. *Cyrano de Bergerac* was one of the plays I was studying for my impending French 'A' level – and trying to revise for it was sending me round the bend. Have you ever tried learning by heart chunks of text that quite frankly you do not *comprenez* even *un petit peu?* Anyway, that's why, when this opportunity came up of a weekend away dog-sitting in suburbia for a friend of my brother Toby, it sounded like just the thing – both for my own and my family's sanity ('Either he goes or I go,' my dad told Toby. I'd just complained for about the hundredth time that his bathroom caterwauling was disrupting my studying.) A nice quiet weekend's revision, you know, it was just what I needed . . . Some chance.

I arrive at the house early Saturday afternoon as arranged. There's a notice on the gate, which reads 'BEWARE OF THE DOG' but I don't care because I know that the dog in question is nothing like the ferocious werewolf depicted – he's a dachshund.

Friendly and cute. No trouble. The only thing I have to beware of is not squashing him underfoot.

I am made a little uneasy by this low, fierce, guttural growl I can hear, coming from the other side of the front door. But I just have to keep reminding myself that this fearsome noise is in fact coming from the throat of a squat little sausage dog the size of a draught excluder. I try calling his name.

'Gandolf,' I call. 'Gandolf.'

I think about rattling the letter box, but decide not to risk it. Better not scare the little pooch.

By the time I put the key in the lock, the growling has turned to a very loud, very resonant barking. I've always thought that dachshunds are rather feeble and yappy, but this one's voice seems long since to have broken. But then, of course, this dachshund, as I should have suspected, is not a dachshund at all. He is, as I spy with my horrified eye on opening the door, a different sort of German dog beginning with 'D' entirely. I step into the house, looking down, in search of something small and stumpy that might possibly chew my ankles, and find myself, an instant later, pinned to the wall, looking up into the black jowly face of the Hound of the Baskervilles. Gandolf is a Doberman pinscher.

For the next few moments I am locked in a desperate struggle with a six foot slavering, possibly rabid monster. My overnight bag goes flying down the hallway as I flail wildly with my hands to protect my face from the jaws of the brute, too terrified to do anything more than shout his name.

'Gandolf!' I cry. 'Gandolf! Gandy!'

I can feel the dog's hot fetid breath on my face and saliva from his flabby jowls dribbling on my hands. Any moment now, I think, I'm going to hear the sound of tearing flesh as his teeth sink into my neck and start to rip my throat out . . .

But it isn't teeth I feel – it's a tongue. A slimy, yucky sort of tongue, but a tongue nonetheless. Gandolf is licking me. Great, slobbery, passionate licks. I am greatly relieved that Gandolf isn't going to eat me after all but the face wash I can do without. I try to recover my composure.

'Gandolf,' I say. 'Down boy.'

Gandolf responds by giving me his biggest, ickiest lick yet. His paws are firmly placed on my shoulders, as though he has chosen me as his dancing partner.

'Gandy!' I cry, firmly. 'Down, Gandy!'

This time, to my amazement, Gandolf does obey my command and I am starting to get the impression that, as far as Gandolf is concerned, his name is 'Gandy' – and that is the only name he is going to answer to. It does strike me that there's something pretty incongruous about calling a massive, six-foot, exceptionally well-fed, potentially homicidal mutt 'Gandy' but, well, who am I to argue? I just wish Toby had warned me of this preference in advance, that's all. But then I suppose that's expecting a bit much from someone incapable even of distinguishing between a dachshund and a Doberman.

The lovely Gandy is now looking up at me

expectantly with slobbery chops and a waggy tail. It is his teeth, though, that most occupy me. They are the teeth of a Texas chainsaw between massacres. Looking into those terrible jaws, I start to wonder whether it's possible that Gandy's mother mated with a shark. Ending up as shark meat is not my idea of a nice quiet suburban weekend so, I decide, it's time to take some action. I've got to find the kitchen and get this beast some real dog food.

The kitchen table, thankfully, is well laden with dog goodies – tins, biscuits, treats . . . It looks like a hound harvest festival. I open a tin of dog food and fill Gandy's bowl. Then, while he's distracted, I sneak out of the kitchen, but the bowl is already about half empty by the time I'm through the door.

I spend the next ten minutes or so breathing deeply and taking stock of the situation. The bed I've been allocated looks comfortable enough; it's occupied at present by a rather vile fluffy pink elephant, but when push comes to shove I can soon get rid of him. The bed's a double too, which is quite a luxury. Maybe things aren't going to be so bad after all, I think. Okay, Gandy's no docile dachshund but, well, he's only a dog, isn't he? At least he won't be booming out Gilbert and Sullivan arias in the bathroom when I'm trying to study. I start to unpack.

Downstairs again, a quick survey reveals the house fully equipped with creature comforts – TV and video, hi-fi and compact disc player, personal computer complete with games but, most impressive of all, is an incredibly well-stocked drinks cabinet. It is this that I am in the process of exploring when I suddenly find myself being wrestled unceremoniously to the ground by randy Gandy, now replete and ready to mate with anything that moves. We roll around for a few moments while I struggle to drag myself free from his pumping groin. A table goes flying, a chair follows, but finally I get to my feet. Gandolf is sniffing around where I was lying with great excitement. There's a patch of slobber on my neck and something even more unpleasant on my trousers. I'm beginning to feel like a suburban sex slave and don't much like it. Gandolf, conversely, likes it very much indeed. His tail is wagging like there's no tomorrow – which, considering the way things are going, may well be the case for one of us.

'Woof! Woof!' barks Gandolf with ardour.

I glare at him. Any moment now, I can see, he's going to start trying to make mad passionate love to me again. There's only one thing for it.

'Time to go walkies,' I say smiling.

Outside on the drive, having finally managed to calm down Gandolf sufficiently to attach a lead to his collar, we are detained briefly by a neighbour.

'He used to be such a handful,' she says indulgently, waving her dustpan in the direction of Gandolf. 'He frightened the life out of my pussy cats. And that lovely white bunny rabbit next door. Poor thing. Now he's so well-behaved, aren't you, Gandy boy?'

As if in protest at this outrageous piece of slander, Gandy suddenly makes a bolt commonwards, dragging me along behind.

In a couple of minutes we are on the common. There's a fair sprinkling of sunshine and hardly a person to be seen. This is more like it, I think. The only drawback is Gandolf, who keeps pulling on his lead like a huge fish straining to free itself from a hook. Further evidence perhaps to support my theory that he is indeed half shark. Eventually I opt for what seems the lesser of two evils and release him. He bounds merrily about as though he's got a massive dose of spring fever. He seems perfectly happy sniffing around in the undergrowth. He leaves me alone. I leave him alone. Bliss. I breathe in the fresh air and stroll, letting my mind pass to higher things. That monumental Gallic conk, for example. I utter a few quotes that I've memorized earlier and try and learn some new ones that I've got written down in my pocket notebook . . .

It is only after I've been strolling for some time that I realize that Gandolf is no longer with me. I look left and right. I call 'Gandy! Gandy!', ignoring the bemused expressions of the few passers-by. Finally, I catch sight of the truant hound, away off in the distance, well out of earshot. There is nothing else for it. I put away my notebook and take off in pursuit.

The common stretches for miles and Gandolf seems intent on covering every single inch of it. He chases one dog after another, all the time staying just out of my reach. I am starting to wonder whether I'll ever catch him – or my breath again – when I emerge from some dense undergrowth to spy my charge up on his hind legs, pinning some poor man to a tree. As I get closer, I see that Gandolf is holding the man's arm in his jaws as though it were a stick or a bone. I quickly grab him and put him on the lead, apologizing profusely. I gaze with consternation at the neat line of purpling puncture marks on the man's skin. I think I can safely say that this is one of the most embarrassing moments of my life. But, alas, there is worse to come.

By the time I arrive back at the house I am far too exhausted even to avail myself of the contents of the drinks cabinet. I certainly don't have the energy to wrestle any more with *Cyrano de Bergerac*. Because of my inert condition, I forget all about the sleeping arrangements of Gandolf, who ends up sharing the bed with the pink fluffy elephant and me. Hardly the most appetising of *ménage à trois* but frankly *je suis* too *fatigué* to give a damn.

I sleep soundly, ignoring the early morning sounds of the Sunday newspaper being torn to shreds by a growling canine maniac and, apart from this, the morning passes without incident. I sit up in bed with my books and Gandolf slumped at my feet. He is quiet and almost tolerable and I start to think that maybe he isn't such a monster after all. Little do I know that he is simply saving his energies for the right moment.

The right moment arrives after lunch as I'm

flicking slightly frantically through my notes, trying with limited success to decipher the scrawl that is my handwriting. There's a banging and barking at the back door which, as I've learned, is Gandolf's sign that he wishes to be admitted. I go to the door and open it. Gandolf is there with a rag in his mouth. Cute. He brings it in and drops it on the floor at my feet. Very cute. Only I can see now that it's not a rag at all – it's a rabbit. A lovely, fluffy, white rabbit – dead and slightly smelly. I remember yesterday's conversation with the woman next door and feel myself starting to sweat with panic. A horrible realization overwhelms me – GANDY HAS MURDERED THE NEIGHBOURS' PET RABBIT! My lunch starts to resurface and I run retching to the bathroom.

A few minutes later I am sitting on the bathroom floor with my head between my knees and my entire life passing horribly before my rapidly moistening eyes. *Cyrano de Bergerac*, a dead rabbit, Gandy and the sudden certainty that I am going to flunk all my exams, and thus my whole life, well up within me. It is the storm after the calm. I am on the verge of a complete breakdown. 'Why me?' I wail. 'Why me?' I have never felt so desperate, miserable and alone in my whole life. I wish I were back home. I wish there were someone to comfort me. I wish that I'd wake up and discover it had all been a terrible dream. I wish . . . I wish these damn exams were over.

I am shaken, literally, from my despondency by

Gandy's huge paw. He scrapes at me insistently, whimpering as he does so. I turn slowly to see him gazing at me. On his face is the most hangdog of hangdog expressions. Ears, eyes, tail, tongue – everything is down. He looks, if it is possible, even more wretched than me.

For some moments we just sit there, staring dolefully at one another. Then, slowly, Gandy raises his paw and offers it to me. It is a classic gesture of apology, sympathy, benevolence – Cyrano de Bergerac himself could not have done better – and I cannot help but smile. A feeble, barely creasemaking sort of smile – but a smile nonetheless. I take his paw and shake it. What happens next takes us both by surprise. Feeling a sudden rush of euphoric affection, I throw my arms around his neck and hug him. The storm has passed and I am still afloat.

Downstairs once more, after a couple of swigs of brandy, I dare to make a closer inspection of the dead bunny. Thankfully, there is no blood or wound to be seen on the animal – just mud. The rabbit, I think, must have died of fright. Gingerly, I pick it up and wrap it in a tea towel. Then, plucking up courage I didn't know I had, I carry the shroud next door. It's the only decent thing to do. I ring the bell – several times. There is no answer. The car is not in the drive. The neighbours are out. I AM REPRIEVED.

Now, at last, my mind starts functioning like the intelligent, quick-witted, unscrupulous human being that I am supposed to be. I stop being wet and decent and become devious, like an Agatha Christie villain. I have a plan. First, I make sure that Gandolf is safely secured in the kitchen. Then I go upstairs and fill the sink with warm water, into which I dip the deceased bunny. I bathe him. I shampoo him. Then I wrap him in his tea towel while I search for a hair dryer. Eventually I find one and give the rabbit a blow dry that would make Vidal Sassoon proud, fluffing out the fur until, apart from the pong and stiffness, little Flopsy seems as good as new.

I take the rabbit out into the garden, climb over the fence and put him back inside his hutch, carefully positioning him so that he appears to be sitting by the door. I stand back for a moment to admire my brilliant cover-up job – no one will suspect that Gandolf was responsible for the poor creature's death now, I think. They'll just suppose he died of natural causes. I return to the house and my books with renewed vigour.

Around four, my studying is interrupted by the sound of the neighbours' car pulling up in their drive. Gandy leaps up and runs to the window. I set my book down and wait . . . Ten minutes later, as expected, I hear a scream – after all, the death of a pet is a terrible thing. What I do not expect, though, is what I hear next. A woman's voice crying incredulously: 'The rabbit's back in its hutch!' Then a man: 'Don't be absurd, dear. Rabbits don't rise from the dead.'

For a moment or two, I am totally and utterly

bemused. Then, as the whole farcical scenario slowly becomes clear, I start to snigger. Within a very short time my sniggering has turned into wild, uncontrollable laughter. The sort of crazed laughter indulged in by the characters of spaghetti westerns just before they blast the hell out of one another. My eyes are wet with tears. It is all too absurd. Life, pets, exams, family, *Cyrano de Bergerac*, Gandy, me . . . all absurd. The universe itself is absurd. I find myself rolling on the floor hugging Gandy, who immediately lies on his back with his legs in the air and joins in. Never have I felt so happy, never have I felt so free. *Jamais. Jamais. Jamais.*

Revision didn't seem such a slog after that weekend. Even *Cyrano*. I felt altogether calmer, cooler, more confident about my prospects. My family and friends could hardly believe the change in me. I'd got my sense of humour back, you see – and my sense of perspective. I mean the exams were important all right, but they weren't a matter of life and death. They'd quickly come and go and I'd still be alive, whatever the outcome – which is more than I could say for that poor rabbit. I could prepare myself but I couldn't predict exactly what would be in the exam papers any more than I could have predicted just what would happen on that weekend with Gandy. That's the way it goes.

'*C'est la vie*,' as that old parsnip-nosed swashbuckler Cyrano certainly wouldn't have said. But, then, he'd never shampooed and blow dried a deceased bunny, had he?

Boxes

The room was stuffy and uncomfortably hot. Even though Alex had taken off his overall, he could feel the sweat damp under his shirt. The trap door above squeaked open and another cardboard box bumped its way down the chute and on to the basement floor. It was sale time in the store and the number of discarded boxes had increased tenfold over the past few days. No sooner did Alex break one box up than another two came hurtling down. They were piled almost roof high in places and in such volume that he could hardly get through to the lift beyond. Still, in a couple of hours time, it would no longer be his problem. Today he was leaving.

He'd taken the job to earn some money during the summer holidays. He hadn't realized, though, it would be quite such hard work. All day long he was busy baling boxes, loading trolleys with slabs of cheese, joints of meat and cartons of fruit to take up to the shop floor. Then there were fittings to move or dismantle, rubbish to collect, errands to run ... By the end of the day he was often too exhausted to go out and enjoy his comparative affluence. Still, at least it meant he'd have plenty of money for his holiday in the Dordogne. This time tomorrow, he reflected (punching his heel through the middle of yet another box), he and his friends would be on their way and Stock Bros would just be a memory.

He heard footsteps in the corridor – the click, clack of slip-on sandally shoes – and a plumpish, pleasant face, topped by a vivid red fringe appeared in the doorway. It was Theresa, one of the shop assistants in the food section. She looked at the piles of boxes and whistled.

'You've got your work cut out, haven't you?' she said. 'You'll never get that lot cleared before you go.'

Alex shrugged. 'It's not as bad as it looks,' he said.

'Well, it *looks* bloody awful,' Theresa said.

It was funny, Alex thought, how old she sounded – mature like the cheddar he brought up from the fridges every day. But in fact she was only sixteen, a year younger than he was. She was already a mother, though, with a two-year-old daughter and he supposed it was that – as well as her manner – that made her seem older.

'Why don't you get that skiver Ben to help you,' she suggested.

Ben was another holiday worker but he'd been commandeered by the stockroom on his third day and had stayed well clear of the basement ever since, except to pop in for the occasional natter.

'It's all right,' Alex said. 'I can clear it.'

'Well if you say so.' Theresa said, unconvinced.

She waved the piece of card she was holding. 'Here's a list of stuff we need brought up,' she said.

Alex took the card and glanced at the scribbled list. He was nonplussed for a moment by the item 'tanjareens' before realizing it was one of Theresa's odd spellings. 'Oh, fruit,' he said, with some relief. He'd been afraid for an instant that it might be meat that was required, which would mean a trip to the cold room. That was the one part of the job that he really hated – going in that gloomy room with its greasy floor and pungent meaty smell, and having to sort through the rows of hanging carcasses . . .

'We need it as soon as possible,' Theresa said. 'The displays are getting a bit low and you know what Mr Grey's like.'

'Yeah,' Alex said. Mr Grey, the manager, was a real stickler for everything being spick and span. He even insisted that Alex wear a tie whenever he appeared on the shop floor – as if any of the customers could care less how the porter was dressed. They didn't even notice he was there most of the time. 'I'll go and get the stuff now,' he promised Theresa.

By the time he'd collected together the fruit order, taken it upstairs and come back down to the basement again, the chute was chock-a-block. He'd have to clear that lot, at least, or else Mr Samuels, the stockroom manager, would be down complaining. He had half an hour until tea anyway, so he might as well get stuck in. He rolled up his sleeves, picked up a small box, ripped it open down the middle, squeezed it flat, dropped it into the baling machine and picked up another box . . . He'd got the box flattening off to a pretty fine art by now. Small boxes, with staples, he ripped; fruit boxes, which were tougher and glued, he stamped on; boxes with tape he slit with a Stanley knife. If there had been an 'A' level in the subject he'd have been laughing. But box-flattening wasn't exactly an integral feature of the English, history or economics syllabuses that he was following.

He was so busy with his thoughts and the boxes that he wasn't aware of the arrival of another visitor, until he heard a voice, singing behind him.

'Don't box me in,' it crooned. He turned, orange box in hand, to see Ben leaning against the door frame, an ironic smile on his freckly face.

'What a mountain,' he said, pushing back his shock of blond hair. He kicked out at a small box in front of him, lifting it into the huge pile. 'You should leave it for the Saturday boys. There's three of them. And anyway it's not your problem anymore is it?'

Alex shrugged. 'I may as well clear as much as I can,' he said. It was a trait in his character that he didn't like to leave jobs unfinished. Once he got going on something he was 'like a dog with a bone', his mother had often said. Others were less polite.

'You're mad,' Ben declared. He hoisted his long body up on to one of the bales of cardboard by the side of the machine and watched Alex flatten another box, then position it carefully in the baler.

'Old Samuels has been in a right strop,' Ben said, kicking his heels lightly against his cardboard perch. 'Just because a couple of delivery notes went missing. He's been grouching and snapping all day. Imagine spending your life worrying about something so sad as a couple of stupid delivery notes.' He shook his head contemptuously. 'I can't wait to get out of this place.'

'Mmm.' Alex agreed, busy with another box.

'It's all right for you, you lucky devil,' Ben said, 'you're practically out.' He picked up an old table knife from the rim of the baler and started to dig with speculative malice into the cardboard beneath him. For a few minutes, they carried on with their respective activities without speaking. Then Ben said enthusiastically, 'Just think, this time next year we'll be getting ready to go away to university.'

'Hopefully,' Alex said.

'Definitely,' Ben said. 'I'll be off. Even if I have to go to the Outer Hebrides or somewhere.' He plunged the knife in deeper. 'Just one more year . . .' he added wistfully.

'Yeah,' Alex said distractedly. University seemed an awful long way off, he thought. He was just looking forward to the next couple of weeks and his holiday in France. There was a whole year more of school and a set of tough exams at the end of it before he could really contemplate university. It was an exciting prospect, though: the freedom, meeting new people, working on things you were really interested in . . .

'I'll tell you one thing for sure,' Ben continued. 'I won't be back here next summer. What a dump eh?'

Alex put another flattened box in the baler and sighed. The breathless heat was very uncomfortable now.

'It's not so bad,' he said, taking off his overall. He'd had just about enough now of drudgery and cardboard boxes, but all in all the job had been okay. It had been a bit of a slog but, well, it had only been for a month.

'I'm gonna get an outdoor job next time,' Ben said.

The baler was full now. Alex pressed a button and a heavy plate descended, crushing the cardboard down. He threaded tape through the empty channels and then opening the machine door, knotted the tape tightly so that the bale was secure.

'I'll give you a hand getting it out,' Ben offered, shuffling down off his seat. Together, the two youths dragged the bale from the machine and rolled if over to the wall. When they'd finished, Ben was breathing heavily.

'*Sacre bleu*,' he exclaimed. 'I'd forgotten what hard work this is. It's a doddle up in the stockroom – apart from old Samuels that is.' He looked around gloomily at the mound of boxes behind them. 'I suppose I'll be back down here next week.' He started to remove his overall. 'May as well get in some practice, I guess.'

For the next twenty minutes or so the two boys

stood side-by-side, like brothers-in-arms, fighting their way through the hoards of boxes – crushing, stamping, ripping, tearing, flattening ... They worked with a kind of manic intensity, each spurred on by the other, turning what was usually a grind into a game. Baling had never been such fun. They had such a good time that Alex was late for his tea break. Five minutes into it, he glanced at his watch and realized. He destroyed the box he was holding then called a halt.

'I'm off to tea,' he said, picking up his overall.

'Yeah, I'd better go back upstairs,' Ben said and he too took up his overall. Looking around them, they saw that the floor, although still obscured in many places, was now scattered, rather than piled with boxes. The way to the lift was clear. 'Not bad, eh?' Ben said with a large smile.

'Great,' Alex said, unusually effusive, as a sudden euphoric rush of holiday spirit surged through him. He was off. Work was done; for a couple of weeks at least, it was all play.

Up in the canteen he sat, as he often did, at a table by himself. He didn't mind normally. It gave him a chance to be quiet and still for a while, do a bit of reading. He loved reading. Anyway, by the time he got to the canteen, the tables always seemed to be full and he didn't go out of his way to squeeze himself in. It wasn't that he disliked the other people, he just didn't really know what to say. He felt awkward in their conversations, unable somehow to make any worthwhile contribution. There was a table of them now, shop assistants – Theresa among them – and a couple of supervisors, chatting, laughing ... He glanced across a little shyly at a sudden outbreak of guffawing and his own high spirits of a few minutes before were doused in this shared hilarity, which made him aware more than ever of his separateness. At that moment, on his last afternoon in the place, he wished that he were not sitting alone and feeling so much apart. He wished he were at that table with the others, sharing the joke, listening to Theresa – at the centre of things now as she generally was – holding forth colourfully about someone she knew, with the worldliness of someone twice her age ...

He was glad to get back to his room in the basement, where he could feel alone without any sense of inadequacy or exclusion – just him and the boxes. A few more had come down the chute in the time he'd been away, but not too many. He reckoned he could clear them okay in the hour that remained. His pace was much less frantic than before, though. His actions were mechanical, dreamlike, his mind not on his work but roving wider to the future.

It struck him how different his life would be from, say, Theresa's. For a short time they had overlapped, working together in this store. But for him it was just part of a holiday. In less than an hour he'd walk away and go on to more exciting, fulfilling things; in another year, with luck, he'd be on his way to university, like Ben had said. He'd have left Stoke Bros a mile behind. But Theresa wouldn't – a single mother, with no qualifications . . . This dull, routine, unadvancing world that he could so freely skip out of, like a frog from a stagnant pond, was hers for good. If he'd been feeling sorry for himself a little earlier, up in the canteen, well, now he felt sorry for her. She was okay, Theresa. She deserved better. She deserved a proper life, a decent future . . .

At a quarter past six, shop floor swept, boxes baled, cheeses and cold meats returned to the fridge for the night, he went up to the cloakroom and hung his overall on the peg for the last time. Even though he was glad to be going, looking forward to his holiday, he still felt a pang at leaving. Partly it was just the kind of gentle fleeting regret that any passing experience might evoke, but there was something more too – a sense of, well, betrayal, guilt at his own good fortune, his freedom. It hung heavily on him as he walked through the unlit shop, exchanging goodbyes, and became almost unbearable when he came to the entrance and found Theresa there, waiting to unlock the door for him. He wanted to speak, to say more than just 'goodbye', but he was completely tongue-tied. Theresa smiled at him, affectionately.

'You'll be back to the grind, then, soon,' she said. His mind went blank for an instant and then it dawned on him that she must be talking about school. 'I don't know how you can stand it,' she went on, with a grimace. 'I couldn't wait to get out.' She shook her head sort of pityingly. 'Still, it takes all sorts, eh?' She grinned.

'Yeah,' Alex murmured, unable to think of anything else to say. Diffidently, he returned her smile, then, with a brief 'bye', he was out through the door and into the street. He didn't look back.

Flesh and Blood

The day Mum went into hospital for her hysterectomy, I was seven days overdue. Once or twice
before, my period had come a couple of days late,
but never a week. I was worried stiff – and sort of
puzzled too. Steve and I had been having sex quite
a lot recently, but we were pretty careful – Steve
always wore a condom. A couple of times, though,
he'd been inside me for a bit before he'd put one
on – which I suppose was risky. But we hadn't had
any mishaps – no burst condoms or anything –
so it hadn't crossed my mind that anything might
happen. Until now . . . What made it worse was that
I hadn't had any of the usual signs that my period
was on its way – heavy boobs, stomach cramps etc.

It wasn't exactly with a happy heart, then, that I
went to the hospital to visit Mum on the eve of her
operation. She didn't look her usual cheery self,
either, which I suppose in the circumstances was
hardly surprising. She did manage a smile, though.

'Hello, darling,' she said. 'How lovely to see you
so early.' I told her I'd come straight from school.

'That was very thoughtful of you,' she said, which

made me feel sort of uncomfortable, considering the state I was in.

'Is everything OK at home?' she asked. 'Are you and your father getting along all right?' I told her everything was fine, trying to sound cheerful. Dad and I get along OK most of the time, but he's got a short fuse and can be a real tyrant sometimes over the tiniest things – like washing up, for instance. He thought I should do it more often.

'What about school?' Mum probed. 'Is everything going all right there?'

'As all right as it'll ever go,' I said. I wondered why Mum was asking me all these questions and if maybe she'd sensed something serious was up. I hoped she had, because then it would make breaking the news to her a bit easier.

Mum took hold of my hand. 'I was thinking today,' she said. 'The last time I was in a hospital bed was sixteen years ago, when I had you.' She smiled gently, then shook her head. 'That was a bloody experience. I hope this one will be rather less traumatic.'

'Was it really as bad as all that?' I asked.

'Worse,' she said. 'Much worse, and don't let anyone ever tell you different ... But it has its compensations, of course.' She looked at me fondly and squeezed my hand.

'I was thirty-eight when you were born,' she said. 'Never mind a mature mum, I was positively geriatric. God knows what that makes me now ... I've never told you this, Karen, but I had three miscarriages before I had you and the doctors told me it was highly unlikely that I'd ever have children. They even advised me not to try. Thank goodness, we did, eh?' She held out her hands to me. 'Come and give me a hug,' she said.

I could sense, while she was holding me, that she'd started to cry. Apart from when Gran died, it was the only time in my life that she'd ever cried in front of me and it felt really strange. I mean, I'd cried in front of her loads of times and she'd always comforted me. What was strange was having the roles reversed – and me being the comforter. It made me feel so, well, grown up. But then it struck me suddenly that in a matter of months I might be a mother myself. I knew that I wouldn't be able to say anything to Mum about it, though. Not now, when she was so upset. And anyway how would it sound, after she'd just told me of what she'd had to go through to have a child, if I said, 'Oh, by the way, Mum, think I might've gone and got myself pregnant by mistake?' I realized then too that I'd got it wrong about Mum sensing something was up with me. The reason she'd been acting a bit funny was because there was something she had to get off *her* chest.

After a little while, Mum let go of me and reached for a tissue. She blew her nose loudly.

'Oh dear,' she said. 'Look at me getting all emotional.'

'It's all right, Mum,' I said.

'It's just that having this operation brings it all

back,' she said. 'All those years when somehow I didn't really feel like a woman. Now, well, it's like having your womanhood taken away somehow. Can you understand what I mean, love?'

I nodded. 'Yes, I think so, Mum,' I said, although in truth I don't think I really did. 'But, well, think on the bright side: you won't have any more periods, will you?' The question was only partly rhetorical, because I still wasn't too clear just what happened when you had a hysterectomy. They took your womb out, I knew that, which sounded bloody awful.

Dad arrived at this point and the sinking feeling came back into my stomach. I suddenly started to feel really queasy. The smell of the supper trays didn't help. I felt hot and flushed and like I might faint.

'Are you all right, love?' Mum asked.

'Yes,' I said. 'I think I just need some fresh air. I'll see you tomorrow. After ... you know.'

'Yes, I know all right,' she said and I kissed her goodbye.

She gave me a hug. 'You're a good 'un, Karen Rogers,' she said.

I had a lot of course work for my English Lit. GCSE to catch up on, so I didn't see Steve that night. But I talked to him on the phone and we arranged to meet the following afternoon after school. It couldn't be for long, he said, because it was his evening for football training – which would have got me really mad, if it wasn't for the fact that

I'd arranged to go up to see Mum anyway. I still wasn't happy with his attitude even so, but then, well, that was Steve for you.

We'd been going out for nearly a year now and, more and more recently, it seemed to me that our relationship had lost its sparkle. The physical thing was still strong, but we didn't seem to talk much any more. It was just the sex, really, that kept us together. Steve was the only bloke I'd ever slept with – I'd been a virgin until a few months before – and when we'd first done it, I'd been really crazy about him. Now, though, it wasn't the same. I enjoyed sex, but, well, it was almost like it didn't matter any more that it was Steve. It was just the sensation I liked, the physical thrill; the emotional side of it had died. I had a strong suspicion it was the same for Steve too.

The more I thought about it, lying in bed that night, the more I knew it was true: that we'd lost something. At the start, sex was like something precious, really valuable; like treasure; now, it was more like ordinary money, pounds and pence – and I'd gone and got myself pregnant through it. I'd let Mum down (poor Mum), I'd let myself down. What the hell was I going to do? I felt so alone and so helpless – and stupid too. I tossed and turned all night, worrying about it all.

Steve hadn't got home by the time I arrived at his place the next afternoon. His mum offered me a cup of tea and we had a little chat – mainly about Mum and her operation. Thinking about that took my mind off my own worries for a while. I was getting pretty fidgety though when half an hour went by and there was still no sign of Steve.

'That boy would be late for his own funeral,' said Steve's mum. 'He's always been the same.' She offered me yet another cup of tea. And then, at last, there was a clunk at the back door and Steve's smiling face appeared.

'Sorry, Karen,' he said. 'I got held up.' He threw his bag down on the kitchen floor.

'Hi, Mum,' he said and gave her a kiss. Then he insisted on sitting down and having a cup of tea before we went upstairs.

It was after six before we were finally alone in his room and I was feeling kind of agitated. He said we had plenty of time – his football practice didn't start till half-past seven.

'But I want to go and see my mum,' I said. 'I told you.'

'Oh yeah,' he said. 'Sorry, I forgot.' He went over to his cassette rack to choose some music – we always had music on when we were together, especially when we were having sex – but I stopped him.

'I thought you wanted to talk,' I said.

'Yeah,' he said, 'I do.' He abandoned the music and came over and sat next to me on the bed, on his precious Tottenham Hotspur duvet. He pushed his hair back off his face and looked at me. He was looking particularly dishy. He took my hand. 'How are you, Karen?' he asked.

'OK,' I said. 'The same. My period still hasn't come.' We talked about this for a bit.

Then Steve said, 'If you are, you know, pregnant, Karen, well you don't have to worry too much. I mean, I was talking to someone at school today about it and he said you can get abortions done on the National Health now. It's not like a big deal these days.'

I pulled my hand away from his. 'You talked to someone at school about this?' I said.

'Only one guy,' he said, 'because I know he's been in a similar situation.'

'So you think I should have an abortion, do you?' I said.

'Well, I can't see any other solution,' he said. 'And, like I say, it's not that terrible.'

'It's not that terrible?' I said. 'Killing an unborn baby's not that terrible?'

'It's just a small operation, Karen,' he said. 'People do it all the time nowadays. I mean it's not as though you were like killing a living thing.'

'Of course it's a living thing,' I said. 'What do you think it's doing now, if it's not living.'

'I mean it's not a proper child or anything,' he said. 'It's just a thing, isn't it?'

'It's a foetus, not a thing,' I said. 'You were one once you know, Steve. Supposing your mum had done that to you. You wouldn't be here now.'

'That's different,' Steve said. 'Mum and Dad were married when they had me.'

'So why don't you suggest we get married then?' I said.

'We can't get married, Karen,' Steve said. I was going to say 'Why not?', but then I realized he was right. I wouldn't have wanted to marry Steve even if it had been a real possibility. When it came down to it, we just didn't have that kind of relationship.

'No,' I said.

For a long minute or so we were quiet. I was thinking about the future. I wanted to do 'A' levels, go to university, get a decent job. I wanted to make something out of my life. How could I do all that with a baby? It was like that one mistake was going to ruin my whole life. I couldn't believe this was happening to me, but it was. It was a nightmare, but I wasn't going to wake up out of it.

We talked for a bit longer but without getting anywhere really. There was a strange sort of physical barrier between us too. Usually Steve was all over me; but tonight he hardly touched me at all. He didn't even kiss me properly. It was like I had some kind of terrible disease.

After a while, he looked at his watch for about the tenth time and said, 'Hey, I've got to go. Football practice starts in ten minutes.'

Then it hit me. I'd been so involved in talking about our problem that I'd completely forgotten about Mum.

'What time is it?' I asked in a sudden panic.

'Twenty past seven,' Steve said.

'Oh no!' I cried. 'Why didn't you tell me before how late it was?'

'It's not late,' he said.

'Of course it is,' I snapped. 'I've got to get to the hospital. I told you, visiting stops at eight.'

'That's early,' said Steve, as though he didn't really believe me.

'Yeah, well, Mum's just had an operation, hasn't she?' I said, feeling like I was going to cry at any moment.

'Look, don't get in a flap,' Steve said. 'Mum'll run you there. I'm sure she will. I'll go and ask her.'

By the time Steve had asked his mum, they'd talked, she'd got herself ready, we'd got in the car, dropped off Steve, driven slowly over to the hospital and, finally, arrived, it was ten to eight. I raced in through the doors and, ignoring the lift, dashed up the stairs. Mum's room was on the fifth floor and when I reached her door, I was gasping.

'Karen,' said Mum, surprised, when I barged into the room.

'Nice of you to make it,' said Dad and he looked furious. 'Where the hell have you been?'

I ran over to Mum and hugged her. She looked pretty tired and pale, but she was smiling.

'Oh, Mum,' I said, 'I'm sorry. I'm really sorry.'

And then I couldn't help myself any longer. I burst into tears . . .

When I got into bed that night I was totally drained. I fell asleep at once, despite everything that was going on in my head, and I slept more soundly than I had for days – though I had some pretty weird dreams. When I woke up, the anxiety was still there, sharp, in my stomach, but my head felt a lot less cluttered than it had been the night before. Things seemed clearer, more resolved. I'd pretty much resigned myself now to the fact that I was pregnant and I knew for sure that Steve and I were finished. That much at least was very clear. I was on my own now. Everything was up to me.

When I went to visit Mum that evening, I apologized again for not getting to see her sooner after her operation – but she said it didn't matter. She said that she'd been very tired anyway.

'Your father didn't mean what he said last night,' she said. (He'd called me 'selfish and ungrateful' – amongst other things.) 'It's just his way. He's been under a lot of strain lately.'

'Yeah, I know, Mum,' I said. 'I just wish he wouldn't go off the deep end like that sometimes and say all those things. I mean, you know I love you, don't you?'

'Of course I do, darling, and so does he.' Mum stroked my hair. I asked her how she was feeling.

'Not so bad,' she said. 'Just tired. Still a woman – and a mother.' She smiled, a weary, weak sort of smile and it suddenly struck me how, well, old she looked. She and Dad were a lot older than all my friends' parents, but Mum and I had always been so close that it hadn't mattered. She'd always been in tune with me, right through my childhood, even as a teenager. She was always interested in what I was in to, but she didn't interfere or try and be really with-it, like some mums. Now, for the first time really, I took in the heavy lines on her pale, unmade-up face and the streaks of grey in her unbrushed hair and saw her for a moment like my friends must have seen her – as an elderly woman, more like a grandmother than a mother. It made me feel tearful again – but not for me, for her. I felt so grateful, so loving, so full of sympathy for what she'd gone through. All those years she'd carried on trying to have me, against the odds. I felt so proud that she was my mum. I threw my arms around her and hugged her tight.

'Hey, steady on, Karen,' she said, laughing. 'I *am* a poor invalid, you know.'

'You're great, Mum,' I said. 'And when you come home, I'm going to give you the best treatment you've ever had, until you're completely better.'

'You'd better be careful what you say,' she said. 'If you treat me too well, I might decide never to get better.'

'You look a bit better already,' I said happily, and she did. She was frail physically, but I could tell that underneath, in her heart, she'd come through this ordeal like she'd come through all the other ordeals before. Womb or no womb, she was really strong my mum. And I knew, then, that I wasn't on my own; I never would be while Mum was around. She *would* understand and we'd sort this thing out somehow, together – mother and daughter, flesh and blood.

For an instant, when I felt the familiar stickiness between my thighs, I was actually sort of disappointed. But only for an instant.

Oblivion

It was half-past three on a Saturday afternoon in October. In the churchyard, behind St Mark's, a solitary figure sat on a gravestone. He'd chosen a corner shaded on one side by a massive old yew tree and on the other by a tall brick wall. It was a bright day, but you'd never have known it in that gloomy spot. Only a couple of hundred metres beyond the churchyard wall, the high street was alive with the sounds of busy shoppers, but with the volume on his Walkman turned up to number nine, Maurice was oblivious to that as well.

Preoccupying his life at that particular moment were very deep, all-consuming feelings of hurt and injustice. The others had gone off to London with Tod's older brother for an all-night party and left him behind. All morning he'd waited for the call, the invitation . . . but in vain. At three he'd abandoned his pride and phoned Tod, only to discover they'd already gone, the bastards. There was plenty of room in the car too. You could fit five with ease in one of those old Fords and they'd have saved on the petrol as well. He just could not understand why they hadn't asked him. They'd gone on and on about it at school on Friday, in front of him, as if he wasn't there or as if they wanted deliberately to torment him.

'What is it with you guys?' he'd wanted to say. 'Am I a ghost or something. Can't you see me here? Why don't you ask me too?' But he didn't have the courage. The words would come out wrong, it would be embarrassing. He'd blush and look stupid, just as he did every time in class when he was asked a question. Besides, if he was the sort of guy who could say things like that, confront them, then they would already have asked him anyway. He just wasn't pushy enough. He was unconfident, useless. It was no accident that he'd chosen to sit in the graveyard. He wished he were dead.

Suddenly, from above the gravestones on either side of his own, gargoyle faces loomed at him, mouthing something which he couldn't hear because of the music. His eyes opened wide and he nearly leapt out of his skin. The faces rose, looked at each other and laughed hysterically. Embodied now, they moved towards him. His shock passed and a sort of fear replaced it. He knew them. Jackson and Taylor. They were in the year above him at school – and they were hard. He clicked off his Walkman and took off his headphones, eyeing the two boys nervously, expecting the worst.

'Gave you a right fright there, didn't we?' said Jackson happily. He was the shorter of the two, but with his cropped hair, earring, leather jacket and monkey boots, he was somehow more menacing than the taller Taylor. *His* black hair was shortish too, but styled, and he wore jogging gear and trainers.

'You was petrified,' Taylor agreed cheerfully. 'You looked like you'd seen a ghost.' This thought brought renewed guffaws. Maurice smiled too, but uneasily.

'Watcha doin' sittin' here any case?' Jackson inquired. For once in his life, Maurice didn't blush. Fear kept his face pale. A few months ago, he'd seen Jackson in action, mercilessly pummelling some poor sucker in the playground, and he had no wish to be his latest victim.

'Just thinking,' he said feebly.

Jackson snorted. 'Just thinking,' he mimicked. Taylor forced a laugh. 'Bet he didn't think he'd see us,' Jackson said.

'No,' Taylor agreed. 'We gave him a shock all right.' The two of them were having a fine time. Maurice hoped their good humour would last. Maybe they'll go away now, he thought wishfully. But they didn't. Taylor leaned his tall frame against a gravestone and crossed his arms.

Jackson nodded at Maurice. 'Wattya listenin' to,' he demanded.

'Just some music,' said Maurice.

Jackson held out his hand for the headphones. 'Let's have a listen,' he said.

Maurice handed him the headphones and the Walkman. He didn't expect to get them back, but at that moment he'd have done anything to placate

Jackson. He was scared stiff. He tried to keep his hands from shaking. Jackson placed the 'phones in his ears with surprising care. Then he found the play button and pushed it. The stereo clicked on. For an instant or two, Jackson's face was blank. Then he grimaced dramatically and yanked the 'phones from his ears.

'That's terrible,' he said, deeply disgusted.

'Let's have a listen,' said Taylor, and he took the set and the headphones. A moment later, he grimaced too. 'Uhhh, gross!' he exclaimed. 'What kind of music's that?'

'Weirdo music,' said Jackson damningly.

'Yeah, weird all right,' Taylor agreed.

'It's Joy Division,' Maurice said, because they were both gazing at him menacingly and he couldn't think what else to say.

'*Joy* Division,' Jackson repeated incredulously.

'More like *Death* Division,' said Taylor.

'Third Division,' added Jackson. He looked at Maurice critically. 'That's depressing, that is,' he said. 'What you wanta listen to that stuff for?'

Maurice shrugged. 'Don't know,' he said. Then he added quickly. 'It's my dad's, not mine. He lent it to me.'

'Doesn't he like you, then?' Jackson joked and his snigger found an echo in Taylor. There was an edge to the laughter that sent a shudder through Maurice. Any minute, he thought, they're going to turn on me.

Jackson took the Walkman from Taylor.

'This ain't bad,' he said and he stuck the stereo in his jacket pocket, looking at Maurice casually as he did so, challenging him to make a protest. Maurice stared painedly, but said nothing. It had been a birthday present from his parents. He glanced momentarily beyond Taylor, but there was no one around, no chance of rescue. He felt helpless, useless ... but more than anything he felt afraid. Inside, he cursed the others for leaving him behind. If he'd gone with them he wouldn't be in this situation – on the verge of being beaten up.

'You got a fag?' Jackson asked with interrogatory directness.

Maurice shook his head. 'I don't smoke,' he said.

Jackson looked disgusted again. He put his hand into his jacket pocket and pulled out a packet of cigarettes. The sudden movement made Maurice flinch. Jackson froze and stared at Maurice with sadistic amusement. Then he raised his hand quickly as if to aim a blow – and laughed as Maurice cowered before him, throwing his arm in front of his face.

'Jumpy ain't yer,' he said sneeringly. He offered the pack of cigarettes to Taylor. Maurice sat up again, red now with humiliation; he'd admitted his fear, there was no way back now.

Fortunately, Jackson's attention was distracted temporarily by Taylor's refusal. The tall youth held out a large hand and shook his head. 'Nah,' he said. 'I given them up.'

'Since when?' Jackson demanded.

'Since I started on the weights,' said Taylor. 'It's bad for your body and your muscles like.'

'Bollocks,' said Jackson. 'Smoking's good for you. It stops heart disease. That's right, isn't it?' He looked at Maurice, demanding his support. Maurice knew that Jackson was talking rubbish, but he wasn't about to say so.

'I don't know,' he croaked.

'Smoking's a killer,' Taylor said. 'It gives you cancer and stuff. Everyone knows that.'

Jackson huffed and then lit up.

He took a long drag and blew the smoke out towards Maurice with a contented sigh. 'Lovely,' he said. 'I can feel my heart beating louder already.' Maurice turned his head away and coughed, which amused Jackson no end.

'I'm going for a piss,' Taylor said and he glided away into the undergrowth.

With Taylor gone, Maurice felt really vulnerable. There was nothing now to distract Jackson. It put the spotlight back on him.

'So,' Jackson said. 'You got any money then?'

'No,' said Maurice, wishing desperately that he had. Maybe then Jackson would have left him alone.

'What nothing?' asked Jackson disbelievingly.

'No.'

Jackson blew more smoke, then shook his head. 'Pathetic,' he said. He stared right at Maurice now, and his light eyes were unblinking, deadly – as though Maurice had done him some unspeakable wrong. Maurice braced himself for an attack.

Suddenly, from the direction of the undergrowth, came a cry of amazement. It was Taylor's voice.

'Oi, Jacko!' he cried. 'Come and have a look at this.'

Jackson got up and nodded at Maurice to follow him. It was his perfect chance to escape, but he didn't take it. It never even crossed his mind. Jackson had the same kind of paralysing effect on him as car headlights are supposed to have on rabbits. He just shuffled timidly through the undergrowth after his tormentor.

The ground was spongy, airy. It felt to Maurice as though at any moment it might cave in beneath his feet and he trod gingerly. His foot kicked against an old stone and he shivered as he realized that they were walking over old graves. Ahead of him, Jackson came out of the undergrowth and then stopped dead. A moment later, Maurice saw why. There was a small patch of turf by the wall, in front of which Taylor was standing. His head was facing away from Maurice and bowed, staring at something on the ground. The same something that Jackson was staring at. When *he* caught sight of it, Maurice opened his mouth wide in a soundless gasp. There on the ground before them, grinning up at them, was a skull.

Taylor was the first to speak. 'Looks like the grave's fallen in,' he said softly, pointing to the earth crater in which the skull lay.

'Or someone dug it up,' said Jackson.

'Some dog maybe,' Taylor suggested.

'Don't be daft,' scoffed Jackson. 'You'd need a spade to make a hole like that. How many dogs do you know that can use a spade?' He moved a little further forward and, as if drawn by a magnet, Maurice followed, still open-mouthed. Jackson pointed at the skull with his cigarette.

'Go and get it then,' he said to Taylor. 'Let's have a look.'

Taylor stayed where he was. 'You get it,' he said truculently.

'All right, chicken,' said Jackson. He put the cigarette between his lips and, leaning forward over the hole, lifted out the skull in both hands. Then he raised it up so that they could all see it clearly.

'Ugly bugger, ain't he,' Jackson said. He turned his head round to face the grinning skull. 'Don't know what you're laughing at, mate,' he said. 'You're dead.'

'Maybe he died laughing,' said Taylor.

Jackson looked at him, then he looked again at the skull.

'Let us in on the joke then, mate,' he said, and he held the mouth of the skull to his ear.

'I wonder who he was,' Taylor said.

'Dunno,' said Jackson. 'Doesn't really matter now, does it?'

Maurice gazed at the skull in Jackson's hands. It did matter, he thought. Jackson was wrong. Once that skull had flesh and was attached to a body, with a family and friends, like him; just as one day he too would be a skull. They all would. The skull was part of a person, wasn't it, a person with a name – even if he was dead.

'We ought to put it back,' said Taylor. 'It's not right.'

Jackson grimaced. 'Bollocks,' he said. 'We're just being friendly. Isn't that right, mate?' He grinned at the skull in a kind of grotesque parody of its own expression. Then he took a last long drag on his cigarette and holding the skull in front of his nose, blew the smoke out through the bony mouth.

'That's gross,' complained Taylor, but he looked sort of amused all the same.

Maurice wasn't amused. The sight of the smoking grinny skull made him shudder. It was horrible, sad, humiliating . . . He saw himself in the skull's place just minutes before – being terrorized by Jackson. It struck him then how terribly lonely it must be to be dead. There you were, stuck in the ground, all on your own, for ever. OK, you probably didn't know you were in the ground because you were dead; but the thought of it was still appalling. The whole thing was awful enough without having some ape like Jackson come along and mess about with you. Make fun of you.

'You oughta put it back, Jacko,' Taylor said. Maurice didn't dare say anything, but he moved his head in an almost imperceptible nod of agreement. Jackson looked peeved.

'Why?' he queried. 'I'm not doing him any harm, am I? He's dead, aren't you, mate?' He tapped the skull gently. 'Besides,' he added, 'it can't be a lot of fun lying down there, under all that earth, can it? If you was dead, wouldn't you rather someone like me came by and had a laugh with you. Gave you an airing like.'

Taylor shook his head. 'If I was dead,' he said, 'I wouldn't want anyone like you anywhere near me. I'd want to be left in peace.'

Maurice nodded again, more openly this time. That was right, surely, wasn't it, what Taylor said? But when his thoughts continued on and he actually realized what that would mean – being left in peace for ever, eternity – it sent a chill through him. Being left in peace, being forgotten about . . . that had to be the worst thing of all. He should know . . . In this graveyard, beneath their feet, there must be hundreds, thousands of people buried that no one ever thought about. Many of them didn't even have gravestones to commemorate them. The lead singer of Joy Division was dead. But he lived on, sort of, in his voice, in his music, in the people like him who listened. These people here, though, were nothing, forgotten, sentenced to unending oblivion. The idea oppressed him.

'Anyway, I still think we should put it back,' said Taylor.

'OK then,' said Jackson, surprisingly amenable and, without warning, he lobbed the skull across to his tall companion. Taylor shrank back but just managed to make the catch. He looked down with distaste at the grubby thing in his hands for a second or two, then quickly lobbed it towards Maurice. He,

111

too, was taken by surprise, but he caught the skull cleanly and, without thinking, tossed it over to Jackson again. A game of catch began . . .

As the game went on, the three players became more daring. They caught the skull one handed, tossed it through their legs, over their shoulders . . . They laughed uproariously, now seemingly untroubled by any thoughts of impropriety. Then Jackson dropped the skull and kicked it, and catch became football, and their laughter was even more uncontained. For a while they had the time of their lives. They dribbled, passed and tackled, turned a gravestone into a goal, kicked and pushed and shouted . . . until they heard the cries of other, angry voices and looked across to see the vicar and another man coming towards them.

They didn't hang around for a confrontation. Abandoning the skull, they ran, clumsy with hilarity, away through the undergrowth, across the graveyard and out into the street – not stopping until gasping, giggling, they came to the fountain in the middle of the shopping arcade.

'That was a laugh,' said Jackson, when he'd finally recovered his breath and composure.

'Yeah,' Taylor agreed. Maurice, still breathless, just smiled and nodded.

When they parted some minutes later, there was a strong enough bond between them for Maurice to brave asking Jackson for his Walkman back. But he didn't put it like that. He knew it would be a mistake to plead, because that would return their relationship to its earlier footing and Jackson, he reckoned, would feel obliged to dig his heels in and refuse. After all, he was still a bully. So just as Jackson and Taylor were about to walk away, Maurice said, 'Oh, my Walkman,' casually, confidently, as if asking for something back from a friend. Jackson stopped and stared at him for a moment. To Maurice's surprise, he kept his nerve; he didn't blush.

'Oh yeah,' Jackson muttered nonchalantly, reaching into his jacket pocket. Then he sort of slung the Walkman at Maurice. 'I still think your dad's got crap taste in music,' he said.

'Yeah, you wanna get yourself some decent tapes,' Taylor added, as a parting shot.

As he walked home, Maurice listened to the Walkman, and the melancholy drone of the long-dead Joy Division singer struck a sudden, deep chord of happiness in him. The music seemed to form a secure sort of bone-hard frame around him – resilient as an ancient skull. He imagined himself telling the others on Monday about his adventure, and the looks of awed amazement on their faces. He felt strong, dynamic, assured . . . These feelings would soon pass of course, but for the moment, out there on the street, with the music wallowing in his ears, he was blissfully oblivious to that.

A Bright Night in November

There's the four of us – Scott, Lisa, Jane and me –
and we've been down the pub drinking. None of us is
legal but we don't get much hassle because we look
old enough. I've been drinking in pubs since I was
sixteen and only ever had my age queried once – and
that was by the landlord of the Dog and Crown
and everyone knows he's a bastard.

It's a crisp evening in November and the moon is
very bright as we walk through the streets towards
Jane's house. The stars are quite faint, there's so much
light around – what with the moon and the street
lights and house lights and car headlights. Scott's
larking about, pretending to be even drunker than he
really is, and leaning all over Lisa, who's not exactly
over steady on her pegs herself. I've got my arm
round Jane and am feeling pretty snug despite the
chill. Scott slopes off for a slash in someone's garden
and all I can hear is the rustling of his pee among the
leaves and then a car comes along the bright street,
slowing down as though it's going to stop somewhere
near us. Its headlights are really bright now and it
suddenly dawns on me that it could well be about to

turn into the drive of the house whose garden Scott is busy watering.

'Oi, Scott!' I hiss. 'Get out of there, pronto!'

The next thing I know, this figure comes flying over the wall and goes tumbling onto the pavement. It's Scott. The car turns into a house further back down the road and Lisa, Jane and I crack up. Then Lisa's conscience gets the better of her and she goes over to Scott to make sure he's all right because he's rolling around and groaning a bit. He doesn't say anything, but as soon as she gets near him, he shoots out a hand and grabs her leg and tries to pull her down onto the pavement as well. She scuffles about a bit and then, in the end, she just collapses on top of him and we all start laughing again.

By the time we get to Jane's we've sobered up a bit. Which is a good thing, because it's late and Jane's parents get pretty shirty about being disturbed once they've gone to bed. The last thing I want is to face an irate Mrs Stevens and have to explain just what I mean by taking her under-age daughter to the pub for the evening. She's a big woman, Jane's mum, and a bit of a dragon. She's teetotal too. Well, she's religious anyway – a Baptist, I think – and never has any drink in the house. And believe you me, I've looked.

Jane opens the door and checks that all is clear and then we creep in after her and I quietly click the front door shut. Jane takes us along a corridor, past a big hole in the ground which is something to do with the building work her mum's having done, and into the back room.

'Better take your shoes off,' she says, which starts Scott giggling.

'My mum'll go mad if you get any dirt on her new carpet,' Jane explains.

Jane's mum has got this shaggy white carpet that, basically, no one's allowed to walk on. She's even covered half of it with this sort of protective see-through plastic matting. I thought at first that this was just a temporary measure, but the carpet's been down a month and the plastic sheeting is still there. It doesn't do a lot for the room's ambience, I must say. We take our shoes off and Scott, as is his wont, holds his trainers up to Lisa's nose for her to sniff.

'All that cheese'll give me nightmares,' she says, pushing the offending trainers away.

Jane goes out into the kitchen to make some coffee and I go over and put on a compact disc. Because it's late at night on a Thursday evening in the middle of November and I'm feeling good, I put on one of Jane's dad's smoochy jazz discs with plenty of mellow saxophone. Then I go and slump in the big armchair. With the music soothing and my best friends around me, it feels really good to be alive. I can't remember the last time I felt so at ease with everything.

'This is the life,' I sigh.

'Yeah,' Scott concurs rapturously.

'Shame about the wallpaper, though,' says Lisa.

And I have to agree. It's brown with some hideous

116

floral pattern. I've sort of got used to it, but I wouldn't like to have to live with it. But then I wouldn't like to have to live with Jane's mum.

After a bit, Jane comes in with the coffee.

'Whatever you do,' she says, 'don't spill any coffee on this carpet. My mum'll kill me.'

'She's dug the grave already,' I say, nodding at the hole in the corridor.

'She sounds like a nice woman, your mum,' says Scott drily.

He's my friend mainly and he's never had the pleasure of meeting Jane's mum.

'She's okay,' says Jane.

'So was Attila the Hun,' I say, 'if you were one of his mates.'

'Don't be rotten,' says Jane.

'Yeah,' says Lisa. 'Show a little respect for your elders and betters.'

Lisa is in the year above us at school. Scott groans. Then he tumbles off the sofa and starts pawing at Lisa's legs and pretending to kiss her feet.

'Oh master,' he says. 'I am your slave.'

'Well, slave, you could get my sex right for a start,' she says, pushing him off with her feet. 'I'm a mistress, not a master.'

Scott falls back theatrically, nearly knocking his coffee flying in the process.

'For God's sake, Scott!' Jane says. 'Behave, can't you?'

'Sorry,' says Scott, looking all sheepish.

I've never known anyone who can cram so many

different expressions into such a short space of time as Scott. His emotions are like plasticine. I don't know how Lisa stands it.

At last, we are all mellow and calm and couply – Scott and Lisa on the sofa, Jane lying across my lap in the big armchair. The lights are low, the music smooth and I find myself thinking warm thoughts about Christmas and how nice it's going to be this year, sharing it with Jane. And that's when Jane starts to tell us this story. It's got nothing to do with anything we've been talking about – at least I don't think it has. It just came into her head, she says.

'Well, tell it to get out again,' says Scott.

'No,' says Jane, 'listen. It's a true story. I read it in the paper this morning.'

'You can't believe what you read in the *Sun*,' says Scott.

'It was in the *Independent* actually,' says Jane.

'Yeah, Scott, shut up will you?' says Lisa. 'I want to hear Jane's story.'

Scott pretends to sulk. We ignore him.

'It was about this young couple – students,' says Jane. 'They were out walking in the Lake District somewhere. Up in the mountains.'

'Mountains? In the Lake District?' Scott scoffs. 'There aren't any mountains in the Lake District.'

'Don't be such a prat. Scott,' says Lisa, 'of course there are. What about Scafell Pike?'

'What about him?' says Scott.

'Go on, Jane,' I urge.

'This couple were on a mountain in the Lake District,' Jane continues, 'when it started to get really foggy. And in a little while they could hardly see a thing. So they started to go back the way they'd come. But they hadn't gone very far when the girl tripped and slipped over the edge and down the mountain a little way and broke her leg.'

'Typical girl,' says Scott dismissively.

Jane ignores him.

'Her boyfriend made his way down to her, by following the direction of her cries. She was in a bad way, in lots of pain, and couldn't possibly walk. So, even though she was heavier than he was, he picked her up and carried her.'

'I'd have left her there,' says Scott. 'That would've got her moving.'

'Judging by your performance out in the street,' says Lisa, 'you'd be the one with the broken leg. And I certainly wouldn't carry you.'

'You couldn't anyway,' says Scott.

'Want a bet?' says Lisa.

'Come on then,' says Scott and he gets up off the sofa. 'Prove it.'

Lisa stands up and puts her hands round Scott's bum. She lifts him about half an inch off the ground then tumbles back onto the sofa with Scott underneath her.

'If you two have quite finished,' I say, 'I'd like to hear the rest of this story.'

Lisa and Scott start to snigger.

'Go on, Jane,' I say. '*I'm* listening.'

'So am I,' says Lisa, wriggling free from Scott's arms.

'I'm not,' says Scott.

'Good,' I say. 'Maybe we'll be able to hear the rest of the story in peace.'

'Well,' says Jane, 'the boy carried his girlfriend slowly down the mountain for hour after hour, stopping and starting until, finally, he came to a sort of cave. He knew he couldn't carry her much further, so he decided the best thing to do would be to leave her in the shelter of the cave, while he went on alone to get help. So that's what he did.'

'And while he was away,' Scott says, 'a grizzly bear came along and ate the girl up.'

'No,' says Jane, 'that wasn't what happened actually. In fact, nothing happened to the girl – she was found by the rescue party and taken to hospital and she recovered okay.'

'What about her boyfriend?' I ask, with a sudden unpleasant suspicion that what looked like being a romantic fairy tale sort of story isn't going to turn out so happily after all.

'He died,' Jane says, 'from exhaustion. They found him, about half a mile further down the mountainside slumped over some rocks. He just hadn't had the strength to go on.'

For a few moments, no one says a word – even Scott is stunned into silence. It's me who's the first to speak.

'That's terrible,' I say. 'Terrible. It's so sad. That poor guy.'

'Yeah,' Lisa agrees. 'That's really sad.'

Scott starts to blub. It begins as a kind of sobbing and soon breaks out into a fully-fledged wail, accompanied by the diligent dabbing of imaginary tears.

'Scott, for God's sake!' Jane hisses. 'Shut up will you! You'll wake up my parents.'

Scott's misery quickly transforms itself into an enormous grin.

'Look at Mr Softy over there,' he says, looking at me. 'He looks like he's really going to start crying. It was only a story, Jason.'

'It wasn't a story,' says Jane indignantly. 'It really happened.'

'Yeah,' says Scott, disbelievingly.

Lisa yawns loudly. 'I think it's time we went,' she says to Scott. 'Now we've had our bedtime story.'

Scott yawns too. 'Yeah,' he says, 'you're right. I've still got my geography homework to do.'

Scott and Lisa get their coats on and Jane sees them out. I acknowledge their goodbyes but I don't get up. Jane comes back in and collects the coffee cups and takes them into the kitchen. I can hear her rinsing them under the tap. Then she comes into the sitting room and goes over to the sofa.

'Now they've finally gone, we can get cosy,' she says and beckons me over.

I get up and go over and sit down on the sofa next to her.

'You're quiet,' she says. 'Is there anything wrong?'

'Just tired,' I say.

She puts her feet up on the sofa and pushes me back with her head, so that I'm half-lying, with my feet on the floor and Jane's head on my chest. Then she looks up. 'Kiss me,' she says.

We kiss and pretty soon I can feel her wriggling around on me, rubbing her groin against mine. Normally my response would be equally passionate but not tonight. It's just not there tonight. That story's taken away all my passion and euphoria. I'm lying there kissing Jane but I'm thinking about that boy and girl on the foggy mountainside. I'm thinking about that dark, impenetrable night and that boy and how lonely he must have felt and how he died. And I'm recalling us out in the bright street earlier, laughing, so full of life, everything so bright. And I wish to hell that I could make some sense of it all.

I feign tiredness, and after a while Jane gives up her advances and just snuggles against my chest. I put my arms around her and bow my forehead so that my nose is touching her hair. It smells smoky from the pub. The disc has come to an end now and the only sound is the hiss of the speakers. It must be after midnight. I start thinking about Christmas again and that girl, and how she and her boyfriend won't be spending it together, how bad she'll feel, how much he must have loved her. He couldn't have been much older than me and he's dead. I imagine for a moment what it would be like, how terrible it would be if Jane died ... and suddenly I feel an almost unbearable sense of loss, like I've never felt before. I hug Jane a little tighter and rest my head against hers – my eyes deep in the smoky, cavern-like darkness of her hair, my tears lost in her hair.